Hinds' carbine in his hands, the muzzle pointing at Cal. 'You're gonna need that horse.'

'Good to see you, too, Glenn,' Cal said. 'Guess you're feeling better.'

'I'm feeling like hell.' Macomber growled. 'Come on, whistle up that black of yours. We'll go join the posse.'

'No!' Eliza came running to them, abandoning the two horses. 'You can't take him back, not now. Cal saved your life, twice.'

Macomber's face flushed red. 'I know it.'

'Then let him go!'

'I'm sorry, ma'am, the law don't work that way. He murdered a man. You can't just wipe that away like it didn't happen. I'll see he gets a fair trial.'

Eliza's eyes sparkled dangerously, but when she spoke her words seemed irrelevant. 'What happened to Seth?'

'He'll be fine. Reckon if I ask, Gallagher will send somebody to fetch him. And before you say it, I know Cal saved his neck too. Would have bled to death if I hadn't tended him as soon as the three of you were out of the way.'

Eliza said nothing, and Macomber was almost pleading as he went on. 'Look, I'll stand up in court and make sure the jury knows what Cal did. An' I'll swear that killing Mort was . . . Hell, I don't know what it was,' he finished, turning furiously on Cal. 'Why d'you do it?'

Cal sighed. 'Wish I knew,' he said.

Macomber gaped. 'Are you loco? You claim you were drunk or something?'

'He's lost his memory,' Eliza said.

'How come?'

'I met up with Hambo and Titch Wilkie,' Cal said. 'Pair of 'em came riding up to the cabin before the Hinds gang got back from Silverlode. They decided the hideout would be a better place without me in it, didn't wait to introduce themselves before they started throwing lead.'

'They're dead?' Macomber asked.

'Feeding the coyotes.' Cal nodded, touching the scar on his forehead.

'Trouble was, this crease sent me crazy. When I came to my senses there were a whole lot of things missing from my past. Including my reasons for shooting Mort Bailey.'

Macomber scowled, shifting his feet a little and wincing. 'Look, we can jaw about this once we're on our way, it's been a long night. Miss Prentice, I'd be obliged if you'd help round up those horses.'

'No,' Eliza said. 'Not unless we're heading back to the valley.'

'What for?' Macomber stared down towards the prairie. The little group of riders were still heading south. 'Guess they didn't hear that shot. Maybe a couple more will fetch 'em.' He pointed the carbine into the air.

'No! Please!' Eliza pulled at his arm. 'We have to get back and talk to Seth. He knows something. Maybe he evens knows why Cal killed that man.'

'Seth? What can he know? The kid didn't reach the ranch until Mort had been dead a week.'

'Yesterday, when we were getting that bullet out of your back, he started to tell me about something that happened the day Cal pulled him from under his dead horse, up on the ridge. Seth's feeling guilty about it, and I'm certain it has to do with his uncle. Please, Sheriff. We have to go back.'

Macomber looked doubtful.

'Mac, you and me have been friends a long time,' Cal said. 'Let's all go to the cabin so we can talk to Seth — that's all we're asking. If it turns out we're wrong then I'll come back to Bannack County, quiet as a lamb.'

'We'll be so grateful — ' Eliza began, breaking off suddenly. 'Sheriff, you were crazy to come riding after us. Look at you!' She pointed at the back of his shirt, which was dark with blood. 'You'd best let me see if I can stop the bleeding, because otherwise you'll be going nowhere.'

'And I ain't got the strength to make a decent job of burying you,' Cal said, summoning up a grin. 'Best do as the lady says. Be real inconvenient you dying just now.'

★   ★   ★

'You did right bringing him back.' Seth Bailey let Eliza help him to his feet. 'If he'd gone on bleeding like that I doubt if the sheriff would ever have made it back to Bannack County. He needs a few days' rest.'

'Lot of damn fuss over nothing,' Macomber growled, but he didn't try to move.

'How about you, Seth?' Cal asked, leaning his weight on the table. The way he felt, a few days rest sounded like a swell idea. 'That bullet hole troubling you any?'

'It's mending clean,' the youngster replied. 'I'd prescribe the same treatment.' He lowered himself carefully into the cabin's only chair. 'And for you, Mason.' Bailey jerked his head towards the bedroll in the corner.

'Well?' Glenn Macomber said. 'You

planning to make a run for it?'

'No,' Cal replied, 'I'll be here when you're fit to travel. Guess I'll go with you and face trial, if that's what you want.' He licked his lips, his mouth suddenly dry.

'What do you say, Seth?' Macomber prompted. 'Mason here thinks you know why Mort Bailey died.'

Before the younger man could answer, the door opened and Eliza walked in. She was pale, struggling under the weight of the sack of provisions she'd taken from the pack horse; even her bright hair seemed dulled by exhaustion. Cal pushed upright to help her but she shouldered him aside, putting her burden on the table. 'I'll fix a meal in a minute . . . ' She broke off, looking from one to the other, sensing the tension between them. 'What's wrong?'

Seth Bailey gave a sudden bitter laugh. 'It was all I ever wanted, to be a doctor. When my pa died I pinned all my hopes on Uncle Mort. I wanted a loan, told him I'd pay him back soon as I could. He wrote saying I could have a job at the ranch instead.' Bailey scowled. 'I hoped I could change his mind, but he was dead and buried by the time I got to the Bar Zee. I didn't know what to do. It was Mrs Bailey who persuaded me to join the posse.'

'Hope?' Macomber looked puzzled. 'She sent you after Cal? That's real strange, the reward was her idea too. She promised to pay if anybody claimed it.'

Bailey nodded. 'She wanted Mason dead. The way she told it, he was too popular, and maybe the men chasing after him wouldn't have the heart to see it through, including you, Sheriff. Whatever happened, she didn't want him brought back for trial. She offered me a thousand dollars.'

'I knew Hope didn't feel too kindly,' Cal murmured, 'like it was my fault she turned her back on me and married Mort.'

Macomber's brow furrowed. 'You

made her a widow, Cal.'

'I know it. But maybe it wasn't only Mort's death she wanted me to pay for. Go on, kid.'

'You know what happened. I came back with a broken leg, and you were still alive.' The youngster bit his lip and looked at Macomber. 'He sent you a message.'

Cal stared at him. Suddenly he could see it all in his head. The sun going down as he lowered Bailey off his back; the kid's pale defiant face. 'Yes! I remember! I wanted Glenn to talk to young Joe, Mort's boy. He was there that day!'

'But you never gave me any message,' Macomber said sombrely, looking up at the youngster, 'and you never told me about Cal saving your fool life that day.'

'I needed that money,' Bailey said wretchedly. 'I stayed at the ranch while my leg was mending, and Mrs Bailey never quit reminding me about that thousand dollars, how it was the only way I'd ever get to finish my medical training. Somehow she made sure the second posse didn't leave until I was fit enough to come along.'

'Is that true, Mac?' Cal asked.

Macomber nodded slowly. 'There was business to see to. She said she couldn't face it alone . . . ' His face was hard as he looked at Bailey again. 'So, you didn't give me the message. But did you talk to young Joe?'

'Yes. Though I never got the whole story, because Mrs Bailey came and interrupted us. And after that she made sure we were never alone again. But I know Mason killed my uncle in self-defence.'

'That's not the way I remember it,' Cal said suddenly. 'He didn't have a gun in his hand when I shot him.'

'No. That was where his plan went wrong. Fate, I guess. He'd set everything up. He asked you to visit him when he knew nobody else would be around. He'd been spreading rumours for weeks about how you were broke, and how you blamed him for the cattle you'd lost in that stampede, when he and his men were taking the stock to the rail-head. It was supposed to look like you went there to rob him, and he killed you in self-defence.'

Bailey gave another bitter laugh. 'Only you got lucky. His gun misfired, and the discharge burnt his hand.'

'He dropped it.' Cal stared unseeingly at the young man, remembering at last. 'That gave me the chance to draw on him. If I'd let him live he'd have found a way to finish me; he couldn't let me tell the truth. I saw the boy looking in at the open window, just as I squeezed the trigger. Jeez, that poor kid.'

'But if he saw you kill his father . . .' Macomber said.

'He heard the whole thing. And he saw his father try to shoot me before I drew on him.' Cal bit his lip. 'Joe climbed in through the window. Said he'd had an idea that something bad was going to happen. His father sent him out with Hope, but he persuaded her to come back.'

'There was no gun anywhere near Mort's body,' Glenn Macomber objected.

'No, Hope came in and took it,' Cal said. 'And she cleaned up the powder burns on his hand. She was ready to swear I'd killed him in cold blood. What choice did I have? I couldn't kill her and Joe. I had to run.'

'But why was she so desperate to hide what really happened?' Eliza asked.

'For money,' Cal replied. 'I wasn't the only one Mort cheated. That 'stampede' almost broke a lot of us smaller ranchers. But there was no stampede. Funny thing was I didn't see it, not till Mort told me. He didn't take his usual crew on that drive, he hired in a whole lot of hands from somewhere up north. And I guess they got a pretty big pay off when he sold the cattle that were supposed to have died on the way. If that ever came out, Hope Bailey would lose every cent Mort left her.'

'I can't let that happen.' Seth Bailey

269

was suddenly on his feet. In his hands was Moke's long-barrelled Colt. He backed up towards the stove. 'I need my share of that money. I need what she promised me.'

There was a moment of stunned silence. It was Eliza who found her voice first. 'No, Seth. You can't do this. You saved the sheriff's life, taking that bullet out of his back. You're not a killer.' She took a step towards him.

'Stay where you are,' he said wildly, both hands on the gun now as he pulled back the hammer. 'Don't come any closer.'

'Or what? You'll shoot me? That's the only way you'll get your hands on that filthy money.'

'Eliza!' the word was a prayer, torn from Cal's dry lips. He was on his toes, his eyes fixed on the weapon, waiting for the faintest twitch of Seth's finger, 'Bailey. Don't — '

The crash of the shot was thunderously loud in the tiny cabin. Cal threw himself forward, gathering Eliza into his arms as she fell back. Seth Bailey flung the gun down and ripped open the door, his footsteps fading into silence as he ran from them, ran from the person he had so nearly become.

A faint wisp of dust drifted down from the roof where the bullet had embedded itself in the dry old wood. Eliza twisted in Cal's arms and pressed her lips to his mouth, pulling free after a long breathless moment to smile at him. 'I told you I could look after myself,' she said. 'And this time I didn't even need a frying pan.'

THE END

We do hope that you have enjoyed reading this large print book.

Did you know that all of our titles are available for purchase?

We publish a wide range of high quality large print books including:
**Romances, Mysteries, Classics
General Fiction
Non Fiction and Westerns**

Special interest titles available in large print are:
**The Little Oxford Dictionary
Music Book, Song Book
Hymn Book, Service Book**

Also available from us courtesy of Oxford University Press:
**Young Readers' Dictionary
(large print edition)
Young Readers' Thesaurus
(large print edition)**

For further information or a free brochure, please contact us at:
**Ulverscroft Large Print Books Ltd.,
The Green, Bradgate Road, Anstey,
Leicester, LE7 7FU, England.
Tel:** (00 44) **0116 236 4325
Fax:** (00 44) **0116 234 0205**

LONG RIDE TO SERENITY

This is a story of murder, greed and corruption littering the long dark trail from the East Coast of America, to south Texas. It is the story of Louise Kettle, a frontier woman, and her love for an ageing gunfighter, a man with a voice in the White House. He is the fastest gun south of the Picket wire, and always behind him is a stone-cold killer on a mission from God. This is the story of the pistolero, shootist and gentleman, Rio Jack Fanning: The Undertaker . . .

HARRY JAY THORN

♦

LONG RIDE TO SERENITY

Complete and Unabridged

LINFORD
Leicester

First published in Great Britain in 2016 by
Robert Hale
an imprint of The Crowood Press
Wiltshire

First Linford Edition
published 2019
by arrangement with
The Crowood Press
Wiltshire

A catalogue record for this book is available
from the British Library.

ISBN 978–1–4448–3982–1

Published by
F. A. Thorpe (Publishing)
Anstey, Leicestershire

Set by Words & Graphics Ltd.
Anstey, Leicestershire
Printed and bound in Great Britain by
T. J. International Ltd., Padstow, Cornwall

This book is printed on acid-free paper

For Keith Overington and our many coffee and cracker-barrel chats in The Contented Pig

Prologue

The old man settled the blued barrel of the Sharps rifle across the saddle of his bay horse. The animal did not move; it was a ritual performed over many years, a common practice on the great buffalo hunts when the mount acted as a shield for the hunter, allowing him to manoeuvre himself into close range of the buffalo without spooking the herd. Sometimes a good shot could down fifty of the giant animals before they sensed the danger and thundered away across the Great Plains. Today though, the old man was not hunting buffalo. He raised the leaf sight and settled it on the distant narrow back of the man in the long, grey duster. He estimated the range at around six hundred yards, allowing for the gentle breeze and the slight rise in the grassland before him. He adjusted his aim very slightly, put a

1

light pressure on the rear trigger to set the cock and gently rested his finger on the front trigger, brushing it, taking the recoil in his narrow shoulder. The sound he never heard reached the distant man a fraction of a second after the bullet struck him in the centre of his back, smashing his spine and killing him instantly. He pitched forward, dead before he hit the ground. The man ejected the brass and popped the hot shell casing into his jacket pocket to be reloaded and used again when the price was right. Then, unhurriedly, he sheathed the long rifle in its leather case and hung it on the pommel of his saddle. He spat into the ground, mounted the animal and made his way down to the unmoving corpse.

The man in the duster was dead, a small hole in the back of his coat but a very large one at the front had the hunter cared to turn him over, and he did. The man could not resist looking into the face, the last second of his victim's life on earth; the face, the startled uncomprehending surprise, the fear-filled eyes of a falling man, dead on his feet. The ritual was part of his fee. The gunman had no desire whatsoever to know the man he had just killed; that he was dead was enough. He picked up the theodolite and tossed it away from the body, following that with other pieces of surveying equipment. He kept the leather map case and its sheaf of maps for his employer and dumped the contents of the saddle bags onto the corpse, then leading the dead man's horse behind him, he set off in the general direction of Serenity, South Texas. He hoped to make it to his cabin a few miles beyond the town before nightfall, well ahead of the dark clouds filled with the promised rain he could smell on the rising breeze, a gentle blow which turned rapidly into a wind and delivered the downpour long before he reached his destination and the promised bounty.

1

Rio Jack Fanning

The angry man walked in through the swing doors of Tom Kettle's place and he was looking for a fight. He was red faced from cheap liquor bought and consumed on the Mexican side of the town. He was weaving slightly but sure enough about what he wanted for the rest of the evening since that Mex whore had laughed in his face when she found him too whiskey-filled to enjoy the five dollars he had paid for her services. She kept the money anyway and that added to his misery, a misery he was intent on sharing.

Kettle's saloon, the Cattleman's Rest, was not overly crowded. A Wednesday night, mid-month, no big spenders on the noon stage and fifteen days to go before the riders of the surrounding ranches found themselves with any folding money in the pockets of their Sunday-best pants.

Two men stood at the bar, their backs to the still-swinging doors. A sprinkling of people sat at tables, two of which were being used for poker with matches for points and one table was being used by a solitary whiskey drummer, playing patience and wondering why the hell he had come to Serenity in the first place. The town certainly didn't need more liquor, that was for sure.

The big man paused, letting the doors bang against his wide shoulders before he lurched across the sawdust floor to the long, dark pinewood bar, reaching it and tossing some coins on to its damp top.

'Whiskey and a chaser, Ryan, and don't drag your ass about it.'

Benny Ryan wiped his big red hands on his dirty apron and reached for a glass, slamming it and the bottle in front of the irritable man. He didn't need trouble or an argument. Wednesday was his early night; another hour and Tom Kettle himself would take over his spot and he could go home, put his tired feet up on the stove and have his own good time with a pipe and a bottle of Irish.

'Here you go, Chet, who the hell shook your tree this evening?'

'Shut up, Ryan, just do what you're paid to do.' A thin, reedy voice for such a big man.

Chet Baker was in no mood for conversation. He turned his back on the tired bartender and looked about the room. One man to the left of him, a tall man, a slight man, dressed in black, high-crowned black Stetson hat sitting on the top of grey hair, overlong and poking out from beneath the brim. A dark moustache. Funny that, thought Baker to himself, grey hair and a black moustache. The man held no real interest for him though. His eyes shifted around the room and finally found what they were looking for. There, right in front of him, not three steps away. A sodbuster, a settler, one of those stinking migrants that passed through each summer and were sent on their way, sometimes with a smile if they listened and heard real good, and at other times with buckshot rattling their tarped wagons if they showed a little deaf. This one must be hard of hearing, Baker thought, remembering the noisy, dirty-faced kids and the wagon with the broken wheel standing by the spring just to the southern edge of the town.

'You,' said Baker, moving across the room and standing in front of the table.

The man looked up at him with moist, weary brown eyes, not afraid, not surprised, simply resigned to the fact that something bad was about to happen. He was small in stature; close-cropped hair; flat, open city face, windcut and sunburned. His clothes were worn; town clothes once, probably smart, but months on the trail behind a team of mules, often crossing dust dry land and dirty water, had taken their toll on the fine cloth.

'Me, sir?'

'Yes, sir, you, sir,' Baker mocked the slight whimper in the man's tired voice.

The man stared up at him but said nothing.

'What the hell you think you are doing in a cattleman's saloon?' Baker pushed it on. 'It's the Cattleman's Rest, what part of that name do you not understand?'

The man continued to stare at the angry newcomer, wondering if a civil reply was going to make a difference in the end and deciding it wouldn't, but went with one anyway.

'Taking an evening beer same as you are, sir.'

Baker stared at him and then without warning, stepped forward and punched the man in the face, hard, knocking him backwards from his chair, sending his beer flying and the man rolling towards the bar. He lay there a moment in the silent room, then staggered to the bar, his feet, his legs caving, his forearm and elbow holding him upright, blood leaking from his mouth.

'For God's sake,' said Ryan, 'leave the man alone.'

'God don't drink here, Ryan, it's a cattleman's saloon,' Baker snapped over his broad shoulder without taking his gaze from the trembling man. He had found what he wanted, he'd show that damned Mex whore. He grabbed a bottle from the bar, smashed it on the hard pine edge and jammed it towards the cowering man's face.

But the raw, jagged green glass never reached its intended target.

As Baker's arm moved down it was grabbed and held from behind. The grip was sure and strong; he turned, trying to shake it but it held firm. The slight grey-haired man was smiling at him. Holding him like he was a child. As the grip tightened his fingers splayed and the broken bottle hit the floor with a clatter, the residue of alcohol mixing with the sawdust in a brown puddle around his dusty boots.

'Goddamn you.' Baker stepped back as the man released him and, turning his back, returned to his chosen place at the bar picking up his beer and taking a deep swallow of the cool liquid as if nothing had happened.

'Goddamn, you, I said goddamn you, old man.' Baker stepped away from the bar, opening his jacket, his hand moving towards the Colt sitting in a tan leather holster on his beefy left hip.

'Wouldn't do that were I you,' said Ryan, quietly, mopping the bar as he spoke.

'I told you already, shut your Irish mouth,' Baker snarled, his hand high, fingers still talloned above his six.

Ryan ignored him, still wiping the already dry bar, rubbing at an invisible spot. 'Don't say I didn't tell you, Chet, that is if you can say anything later on at all. That there man you are aiming to gun down is not the kindest man I know.' He nodded casually towards the grey-haired man, who seemingly had no interest at all in what was going on just

11

five yards to his left. 'That *old man* is Jack Fanning, sometimes known as Fanning John or Rio Jack, depending on which side of the border you ride.'

There was a murmur, a ripple of sound around the room.

Tom Kettle had just entered the bar from out back in the store room. He froze, feeling it; he leaned his scrawny old body against the door jamb, the cold moving through the room, the feeling you get when an undertaker brushes by you. A graveyard chill. He knew that Rio Jack Fanning was also known as The Undertaker — and that was on both sides of the border.

Fanning did not move, his tanned face expressionless under the dark brim of his high-crowned black hat, the grey eyes fixed somewhere off in the middle distance, his slim body still beneath the lightly threadbare black suit.

Baker stood as if turned to stone, staring at the man's narrow back, wondering for just a moment if he could take him, a fleetingly foolish thought but a real one nevertheless.

'You would never make it, Mr Baker, not on your very best day.' Fanning whispered the words into his beer without turning. The voice like a cold winter's morning, soft and bitter; still leaning on the bar, his drink inches from his lips.

Baker lowered his arm, tried to speak but his mouth was dry, the words catching in his throat.

Fanning said, 'Buy the man a drink, help him to his table, dust him down and tell him how sorry you are for roughing him up. That will take care of it as far as I'm concerned. You got another way, then get it done, you're ruining my evening. Touch that Colt though and you are in for a whole lot of bad.'

Baker gagged again but did as he was told. Turning, he helped the farmer back to his table, set the chair straight and dusted the man down, patting at his soiled threadbare clothing, helped him onto the chair and tossing some

13

coins on the bar, took the schooner of beer Ryan poured and set it before the startled man. 'Sorry I hit you . . . ' The words tailed off and he began to turn, thought better of it and walked from the bar, the doors swinging mockingly behind him and the chuckle from the card tables lifting the room, warming it again. Baker was not a popular man, even among the townspeople with whom he shared a drink from time to time.

Kettle sighed and stepped back into the stockroom, thinking was this a good day or was this a good day? He smiled to himself; it was indeed a good day if it went well.

Ryan moved along the bar, still wiping it, then standing in front of Fanning. 'You want another beer, Jack?'

'It wouldn't hurt any,' said Fanning, 'this one's gone flat. Do I know you, Ryan?'

'No, sir, not exactly. I worked the Shell House Bar in Walkersville where you shot and killed Bucky Nelson and his no-good brother Harold, six or seven years back. You cost me twenty bucks that night. They had been running a slate for two weeks before you showed and the town marshal said they didn't have a dime on them when you put them down. The county took and sold their trappings to bury them and I ended up on the short end.'

'Sorry about that, Ryan.'

Ryan smiled; the man sounded like he really meant it. 'Not so bad really, I bought the four slugs the doc took out of them no-good bastards for two bits each, matched them with the brass you shucked when you reloaded your six in the saloon and sold 'em to a drummer for ten dollars. He sold them to a travelling show back east and we all made money.' He laughed. 'Damn it, maybe I should have let you put a couple in Chet and sold them as well.'

Fanning smiled, stepping away from the bar, opening his coat. 'Now that would have been something to see,

Ryan, I'm not packing.'

Ryan stared at the man's waist. A polished leather pants belt with a silver buckle was all.

'Jesus, yes, that would have been something. You really want to die that bad, Jack?'

'Man carries a gun all his life, he's bound to end up getting shot sooner or later, whether he's heeled or not on the day.' It was a thoughtful reply, like it was a long considered one. Like he had thought about it long and hard on dark nights on cold trails or in cheap hotel rooms.

'Yes, I guess a man like you is likely to get shot packing or no.'

Fanning smiled. 'Bucky Nelson, that was a while back and Montana is one hell of a ride from Texas, Ryan.'

Ryan shrugged. 'Like gunfighters, bartenders move along.'

'You moved a hell of a way.'

'In front of you or behind you, we both made it to Serenity.'

'I'm just passing through — you look

like you are set behind that bar for a spell.'

'Part owner. Where you headed?' The two of them like old friends, a warm evening and little else to do but chew the fat about old and better times. Neither man noticed the door to the store room cracked or the shadow of Tom Kettle.

'There's a little town called Sawcross, east of Del Rio, needs a badge — they offered it and I took it. Good fishing I hear. It's not what it was, not too many around like Baker wearing their gun outside their pants these days, but border towns are cranky and it will do.'

'I hope you make it,' said Ryan, dipping behind the bar and coming up with a blue steel Colt. He set it on the bar in front of Fanning. 'You might need this when you go out on the street later. Chet Baker isn't a man to let something like what happened here tonight pass him by.'

Fanning shrugged and grinned a friendly smile; almost boyish had it not

17

been for the coldness that lay smouldering around the edges of his mouth.
'Men like that are all wind, Ryan. He'll
sober up and get along home thinking
to himself of how he faced down old
Jack Fanning and when I'm gone from
here he will brag on it.'

'I don't think so, Jack. Baker rides for
Sam Colston's Broken Bow, that's the
biggest spread around here and he can't
afford to lose face. Broken Bow is
important to him and Chet wouldn't
want Sam Colston thinking anything
less of him. It's a dark night, no moon
to speak of. Take the piece anyway. You
don't need it, then drop it by in the
morning before you leave and I'll stand
you a coffee.'

Fanning picked up the Colt revolver.
A companion to his own favoured
sidearm. An army model .45 with a
six-inch barrel, gutta-percha grips. He
flipped open the gate and turned the
cylinder, listening to the smooth click of
the ratchet. Five brass-capped ends
with an empty chamber under the

hammer. He hefted it, enjoying the moment, aware that all eyes in the room were on him. He spun the gun on his trigger finger, flipped it and handed it grip-first to the smiling Ryan who knew what was coming but who reached for it anyway, only to see it flip and turn, the round muzzle resting on the front of his dirty apron.

Fanning asked quietly, 'You really think he's out there waiting for me, Ryan?'

'I'd bet money on it . . . '

Fanning set the gun on the bar, suddenly aware of the slight, balding man standing on his left.

'Evening, Tom, you missed the excitement,' Ryan said, beaming. 'Jack, this is Tom Kettle — he owns most of the place. Tom, this is Jack Fanning, late of anywhere north of here, I guess.'

Kettle stuck out his hand and Fanning took it, surprised at the thin man's firm grip.

'Nice to meet you, Mr Fanning, heard a lot about you one way or another. I also heard what Ryan told you — he's very likely right about Baker.'

'Would you like a coffee, Dad?'

The voice was soft and Fanning smelled her before he saw her. A tall auburn-haired woman; hazel eyes, the slightest of overbites, soft lips with tiny lines running down from high cheek-bones. Early thirties he guessed, not a beauty but handsome, the best-looking woman he had seen in a long while.

'Thanks, honey,' said Kettle quietly, then, 'Mr Fanning, meet Louise, my daughter. She takes care of me and just about everything else around here.'

Fanning removed his hat, revealing a shock of untidy grey hair. He bowed his shoulders briefly, held her eyes a long moment before she averted her gaze, her cheeks flushed with colour, just noticeable under the flickering light from the oil lamps. 'A pleasure, Miss Louise, a real pleasure.'

The woman smiled and looked at Kettle, still awaiting an answer to her question, seemingly dismissing Fanning.

'Yes please, honey, and maybe our visitor here would like one.'

'No thanks,' said Fanning. 'Keeps me awake. I think I'll head back for the hotel, it's been a long day.'

She smiled and walked back across the room to where the stairs linked the bar to the upper living quarters. She glanced back at the three men briefly and disappeared from view, moving gracefully up the stairs, her long, black skirt brushing around slim ankles.

Fanning smiled at Kettle, thanked Ryan for his hospitality and moved towards the swing doors, stopping suddenly in mid stride and, turning back to the bar, he picked up the Colt. 'You could be right, Ryan, I've never known a bartender who wasn't.'

Holding the long-barrelled Colt at his side he moved back across the room, paused for a moment at the swing doors before stepping swiftly through them and to his left. A muzzle flash leapt out of the darkness between two buildings on the opposite side of the street and lead splintered one of the swing doors. It was followed quickly by another. Fanning heard the sound of breaking glass and hoped Ryan and Kettle had ducked. Then the borrowed gun was bucking lightly in his right hand as he poured two quick rounds at the muzzle flash, then again moving to his left and pumping two more into the same darkness of the alleyway. Above the crash of the gunshots he heard the scream of pain and anger, but he held fire and the hammer cocked over the last round.

Baker staggered out of the darkness and into the dimly lit street, there was blood on his shirtfront and his gun was dangling from the limp fingers of his right hand. He sat down hard on the boards of the sidewalk, then dropping the gun and holding his side with both hands, moaned mournfully like a wounded animal.

Fanning lowered the hammer and

walked across the rutted street, Kettle, his daughter and Ryan overtaking him, reaching Baker, propping the wounded man against the veranda upright. Louise took charge, yelling for someone to get Doc Henderson before Baker bled to death, her voice bouncing back from the darkness, strong, commanding.

Fanning, his ears still ringing from the gunfire, knelt down. Baker had been hit three times; his whole left side was blood-soaked. Hits through the left shoulder, thigh and an ugly raw bullet crease just above the hip bone, bad but not necessarily fatal. He straightened and handed the smoking gun to Ryan. 'Pulls to the left, lucky for him. You got any kind of law around here needs knowing this? I wouldn't want to leave town tomorrow and find paper on me somewhere down the line.' He straightened and leaned against the hitching rail.

Doc Henderson, a fat man in a flapping nightgown, pushed the men aside and bent down to examine the white-faced Baker, then yelled instructions to his equally fat wife and a couple of loafers to get the wounded man down to his office.

'You know what they say, Jack,' Kettle eventually said in answer to his question, 'no law west of the Pecos and certainly none to speak of in Serenity. We don't rate a county deputy at present, only a constable, but he's deaf and wouldn't come out in the dark anyhow. I'll see it's reported just as it happened to Sam Colston, he's about the only law around here at the moment although that will change. You want a nightcap?'

Fanning smiled a tired smile, the movement of the muscles crinkling his eyes taking ten years from off the weariness that besieged his face. 'No thanks, I'm beat, thinking of getting an early start in the morning. Goodnight, gentlemen, ma'am.' He touched the brim of his hat and then he was gone, swallowed up in the darkness beyond the reach of the flickering oil-filled street lamps as if he had never been.

Kettle shivered and taking Ryan's arm, walked back across the street to the saloon, wondering was tomorrow going to be the good day he hoped for.

★　★　★

Fanning needed the nightcap badly and was glad the darkness had hidden the fear behind the practised smile. His hands were trembling and he thought that perhaps the woman Louise had noticed, but then again, maybe the darkness had hidden that as well.

2

The Badge

'He's a cranky old bastard, what makes you think he will go for it? Excuse me, Lou,' Ryan nodded to the woman who smiled and shook her head.

'How old is old?' Kettle said, thinking about the answer himself.

'He would be around forty-three, forty-five.'

'And that's old?' Louise asked.

'It is in his profession,' Ryan said quietly, 'too damned old.'

The three of them were sitting around one of the polished card tables in the empty saloon, the two men with schooners filled with flat beer in front of them, the woman with a cup of coffee. The batwings stilled for the night, the outer door locked. The room smelling of stale alcohol and cigarette smoke, all but one of the oil lamps turned down, smoking wicks adding to the clogging atmosphere.

'He looked pretty tired to me,' said Louise. 'More worn out than old.'

'He's been around some,' said Ryan. 'A stint on Pennsylvania Avenue, Deputy US Marshal in Wyoming with Brubaker. An elected officer in Montana, a town marshal, Pinkerton man. A bounty hunter but mostly behind one badge or another, although they do say he has stepped out from behind it now and then if it suited him. He's well known south of the line.'

'Has he ever been married?'

Ryan looked at Kettle, then at the woman and grinned, 'No I guess not, he's too damned smart for that.'

'Smart or not,' said Kettle, still thinking about old age and wondering where that put him in the scale of things. If forty-five was old, what then was he? 'Smart or not,' he repeated quietly, 'he damned near walked out on that street naked tonight and were it not for Benny here, he would most likely have got his head shot off. No. He's a tired man and my guess is he's looking for somewhere quiet to bed down permanent.'

'And you think that's here in Serenity?' Louise asked, studying her father intently.

'You don't?' He snapped the question back at her.

'There is something very dark about the man — he talks light, but he thinks heavy,' Louise said, her voice little more than a whisper. 'He looks like a man who would rather not ride another mile if he could avoid it. Do they really call him The Undertaker?'

'It is not an uncommon sobriquet, and such names stick out here,' Kettle said. 'It's a fact of life.'

⋆   ⋆   ⋆

Fanning sipped the fresh morning coffee then set the cup aside and forked eggs onto the ham, sliced it and ate methodically. He was not hungry. His back hurt a little from a restless night on a hard bed and he was forced to acknowledge to himself, as he had on more than one occasion over the past year, that he was no longer a young man. Brawls in grubby smoke-filled saloons, gunfights on dark streets, too much beer and whiskey on an empty stomach and a greasy breakfast in Serenity's Red River Café were not things he could any longer take in his stride. He thought of the long ride ahead of him to beyond Del Rio, the hard saddle and a strange horse and the morning seemed a whole shade greyer to him than in reality it actually was. The early morning sun was trying hard to burn the damp from off the breeze that drifted down from the hills surrounding Serenity and begin the day-long task of warming the West Texas air. He pushed the plate to one side and returned his attention to the cooling coffee. It was good coffee. A shadow settled lightly on the table and he looked up into the thin, weathered face of Tom Kettle. He nodded to the saloon owner.

'Mind if I join you, Mr Fanning?'

Fanning pushed a chair out with his booted foot and signalled to the red-haired waitress for more coffee. She smiled and vanished into the kitchen behind the long empty counter. The saloon was almost empty. 'Help yourself, the coffee is only half bad.'

'I know, I own the place.' He smiled. 'This and two thirds of the Cattleman's, Ryan has a third stake in the place and I own one of the two hardware stores, the tack shop when it's open and the *Serenity Sentinel* when I get the time, though Louise takes care of that mostly and I also have a part share in the livery. Oh, and I am also the mayor.'

'Big man in this town, Tom Kettle. How come you don't have any law worth a damn?'

Fanning's thoughts drifted back to the previous night and the fact that there was no badge to report the attempt on his life and the self-defence shooting that followed.

Kettle nodded his thanks to the redhead, who swished up to the table and deposited a fresh steaming pot of coffee before the two men. 'Thanks, Anne, Jack Fanning here thinks our coffee is only half bad, he didn't say anything about the grub though.'

Fanning blushed and smiled at her through it.

The woman grinned back at him. 'Well, Tom, he sure enough ate it all.' She chuckled and swept away. The second handsome woman he had seen in Serenity. He wondered vaguely, were there any more?

The only other customers, two young cowboys in worn range clothes, pushed themselves away from the café's dining counter and headed for the door, roweled spurs jangling, both glancing at the two men as they passed by, the older of the pair nodding at Kettle.

Kettle poured himself a cup full to

the brim, sugared it generously and stirred a little cream into the dark brew. 'Law was what I wanted to talk you about, Jack,' Kettle said quietly, the pleasant interlude with the redhead seemingly forgotten. 'All right if I call you Jack or do you prefer Rio?'

'Jack will do just fine, the Rio part Ryan mentioned is for south of the line, it's not a handle I chose for myself.'

'I would guess there are lot of things in your life you didn't choose for yourself, Jack, and maybe I want to offer you a choice here and now in Serenity.'

Fanning wished he hadn't quit smoking. A quirly would go down well right about then, he thought, waiting for the old man to get to the point — if there was a point.

'You asked me about law in Serenity. Well, we don't have any real law at present. We did have one time, a town marshal. Joe Rivers was a decent enough man, fell off his horse and drowned in Saddlebrook Creek, drunk they said although he was never known to indulge. Deputy took over for a while but he broke his neck when his horse was startled — by a rattler, so they reckon. It seems our lawmen were born to bad luck or were not the finest of horsemen in South Texas. It's a wide-open town at present. The election for the Belstone county badge is in a couple of months and then things might change, although they may not necessarily change for the better.

'We don't rate a deputy sheriff now and I cannot see that changing. What you witnessed and inadvertently became part of last night was pretty much the norm around here. Cattlemen led by Sam Colston and squatters smouldering, snarling at each other, pretty soon snapping and biting and then there will be killing. It must be familiar to you as a lawman. The land will be worth a fortune if the South Texas Railway Company decide to take in Serenity as a route to Belstone.' Kettle's voice tailed off, like he was thinking of sometime, someplace, long ago.

'And if they don't choose the Serenity route?'

'Then they will take the Colfax trail, I don't see as that will do Colston any favours though.'

'Are you sure you are getting the whole picture here? This trouble you are expecting could well persuade them to avoid a hot spot like Serenity with a range war brewing.'

Fanning finished his coffee and took a deep breath, moving his chair back an inch, impatient. 'But what's your real point here, Tom? You appoint a local man, a good man who can sit between the two. Old times are over, range wars done, I have been here two days and I do believe the only man I saw packing was that yesterday's leftover Baker last evening. It's getting quiet around here and the same all the way back up to Wyoming and Montana.'

'In a way you are right, but not quite. We are a little pocket of darkness here with the cattlemen not quite as ready to give up any of the government land as they may have been up north. Sam Colston is a law unto himself and he will, although he may not know it, hold this corner of Texas back a decade. In that time the railroad will pass us by, go on to Colfax and Belstone and we will be forgotten and that is all wrong. Serenity needs to grow, it can grow, become something, a place to be proud of. We keep the farmers and the ranchers apart, clean up the town, don't blow the lid off, we have a great future if the railroad pushed through here but they will steer well clear if the town stinks of gunpowder. We slip into gunfights and murder and we will become the backwater we deserve to be.' There was a sudden passion in the old man's voice, a fire dancing in his rheumy eyes and his hand trembled as he picked up his mug and drank deeply from it.

'So get the right man appointed,' Fanning said quietly, suddenly wanting to be gone from that place.

'It will be Sam Colston's man and that's for sure, unless the town council choose someone to take the job. Colston thinks he owns us but he is wrong there. We need someone the townspeople trust, a man the settlers can see is not saddlebound, a man who doesn't stink of beef.'

Fanning felt irritated knowing what was coming and not wanting to hear it.

'Ryan tells me you have a badge offer down south by Del Rio, a quiet town with good fishing.'

'Bartenders always talk too much.'

'That may be so, but is it true enough?'

'Something like that.'

'Well consider this, Jack, there are some big mouth bass in the clear waters of the foothills less than a half hour's ride from here. The town will be quiet with the right man behind the shield and we will triple whatever down south offered you.'

There it was, out in the open. Kettle sat back and fixed him hard with eyes that held the hint of a smile.

Fanning said nothing.

'You thinking about it or what. Jack?'

'Why me?'

'Why not you?'

'You want me or my Colt?'

'You, Jack. You come with a good rep as I understand it. You served as a deputy US Marshal in Wyoming under Jack Brubaker, a man I would trust with my life. You've worked county law, town law and I know for sure you were attached to the Pennsylvania Avenue staff for two years. Hell, I have a feeling that behind any piece of tin you are a born politician. Who knows, county sheriff one day, governor maybe, even The Whitehouse . . . ' His voice trailed off. 'Well, a county badge is a good start. You are no spring chicken it is true, but you are far from over the hill.'

'Thanks for that.' Fanning couldn't help the smile. He liked the old man. 'President? Who the hell would ever elect a Texan as President?' He paused. 'And how the hell do you know so much about me anyway?'

'Well, maybe I let my enthusiasm carry me away a little. Ryan has sort of followed your career. Seems he made some money out of you one time. You are right, bartenders do talk too much.'

★　★　★

'Am I disturbing you, Mr Fanning?' The words were softly spoken, almost part of the early morning breeze that drifted down from the distant foothills that bounded Serenity. Fanning turned, shifting his attention away from the big sorrel horse that pawed the dusty beat-up ground beyond the section of corral fence upon which he had selected to lean. He touched his hat, briefly conscious of his freshly-trimmed dark moustache and the shave he had gotten that morning after breakfast with Tom Kettle.

'Morning, Miss Louise. No you are not disturbing me one little bit.' He grinned at the way that sounded.

'Lou, please call me Lou, most everyone does.'

'Lou it is then. Morning to you, Lou.'

She moved up beside him, aware that they were of an equal height. 'He's a fine animal, you thinking of buying him?'

He looked at the horse for a moment and then off in to the morning haze, towards the south and distant Del Rio. 'I don't think so. He's a handsome one sure enough, but to tell the truth, Lou, I am not partial to horses. Mostly they are mean spirited animals and I find riding them long distances to be no pleasure at all. Horses long ago convinced me just where a cowboy's brains are situated and it isn't under a fancy hat.'

'Then it will be a long coach ride to Del Rio and the border for you, Mr Fanning.' She smiled around the words.

'Jack. Jack is good.'

She moved closer to the pole corral and rested her chin on her freckled forearms as he had been doing when she had first approached. The animal stopped pawing the ground, glared back at them and then moved closer, stopping a yard from the rail, staring at them. 'He'd eat you if he could,' said Fanning, meaning it.

'Oh I don't think so, Jack. Here boy,' she reached out her hand, opened it slowly and the animal's ears flipped back at the sound of her voice. He moved towards her, his whiskered muzzle snorting the pony nuts from her open palm.

'And their friendship is cheaply bought, a handful of grub and the damned thing is a friend for life. You known him long?'

She turned from the sorrel and smiled at him. 'About five years, he belongs to Dad.'

'Most everything in this town seems to,' Fanning said, his grey eyes still creased with the hint of a smile.

'Why did you turn him down?' She turned to face him but he kept his eyes fixed on the horse.

'I didn't turn him down, I turned down the badge.'

'Why? He tells me you are on your way to Del Rio to take up just such a job.'

'Sawcross, east of Del Rio and it's very different.'

'How so?'

'Well, it's a one-dog town with maybe a few drunks on a Saturday night or some border trash to move along. Here? Here you have the beginnings of some big trouble — maybe not a war but big trouble nevertheless, the seeding of distrust and the county man will be caught in the middle, come harvest time he'll have his hands full. The rangers may take an interest but I doubt it, they are pretty busy down along the border right now.' He turned to face her and she met his grey eyes with hers, matched the intensity.

'That farmer last night. I don't know him, who he is, who he was or wants to be. Should I put my life on the line for him?'

'You did last night.'

'A foolish gesture, should have kept my nose out of it, damned near got my head blown off, twice.'

'Twice?'

'Yes, once in the saloon when I called him out and once on the street when he took a shot at me. That farmer may be a right Christian and come from a good family but he sure as hell wasn't worth dying for.' He thought about that for a long moment and added, 'And maybe he wasn't worth killing for either.'

3

Broken Bow

Colston crossed the short distance from the large tree-shaded stone ranch house to the squat, wood-built bunkhouse in long easy strides. A tall, slim man dressed in a tired cord jacket and brown wool pants. Hatless, his grey hair swept straight back from a high forehead, his long effeminate face lengthened even more by the pointed goatee. His upper lip was clean-shaven; at fifty-five years old he had long ago given up trying to grow a decent moustache.

The interior of the bunkhouse was dark, dust-speckled rays of light filtering through the dirty windows. One of the beams illuminated the bunk upon which lay a heavily bandaged Chet Baker, his broad back propped up with pillows. Baker nodded and Colston pulled up a wooden chair, turned it, sat astride it and, leaning his chin on his slim hands, stared at his foreman.

'You OK?' asked Colston reluctantly, as if there were no escaping the inevitable question.

'Damn right I'm not, boss. Had two slugs taken out of me and a burn across the ribs hurts like hell.' Baker's reedy voice was low, surly.

'I hear it was an old man took you.'

'You heard wrong then, he wasn't that old and he didn't take me.'

'Took your piece away though.'

'It wasn't my gun, it was a bottle.'

'Beat you over the head with it.'

'He didn't touch me, not then.'

'Kicked your ass out of Kettle's place.'

'Sonofabitch.'

'You laid for him in the alley after?'

'I was mad as hell and a little drunk.'

'And you still missed him.' It wasn't a question.

'He came out shooting.'

'Not the way I heard it.'

44

'Then you heard wrong.'

'Whatever.'

'That's the way it was.'

'Know who he is?'

'No, a stranger passing through,' Baker said, 'looked like he could be John law, a drummer maybe, dressed in black. I guess he's long gone by now though.' Baker lied easily.

'A drummer can puncture you with three rounds on a dark night on a poorly lit street over a distance of twenty yards? Some drummer.'

'Just lucky.'

'And gone? No, Chet, as I hear it he's in solid with our mayor, they had breakfast together at the Red River, could mean trouble. I doubt much trouble but I don't need it. I had you down for the town marshal's shield until the election later in the year, after which we might get a real deputy sheriff. As mayor, Kettle could have done that, though now I don't know.'

'Damn,' said Baker, 'I would have liked that.'

Colston ignored him, getting to his feet and walking over to the window on the south side of the bunkhouse. 'Now maybe I will tell him to appoint Kip Tullet, Kip for the badge and his brother Jason for deputy, should be a good combination. You can join them when you are on your feet, you lazy bastard.' Then, grinning to himself, he left the bunkhouse to the dust and Baker to his pain and misery. Tullet was probably the safer choice anyway. He would ride into Serenity at sundown and tell Kettle what he had decided.

★　★　★

The young cowboy's name was Howard Smith, he was twenty-two years old and of German origin, dropping the 'Smidt' for the more Americanized spelling. He owned a painted pony he called Dodger, a worn-out saddle and a brand new Colt .45 Frontier he packed in a thigh tied-down tan leather holster. He had ridden for Sam Colston's Broken

46

Bow for six months. He was good with that Colt. He could ride and rope as well, if not better, than the top hand and bad weather never bothered him. He could eat his share of steak, beans and trail slop without complaint, but he wasn't then and never intended to be a forty-dollar a month cowboy. He had his sights set on higher things and he believed that Chet Baker getting himself shot up and his own chance encounter and subsequent eavesdropping at the Red River Café would help him on that long road, give him a short cut to Sam Colston's ear.

Jason Tullet, top hand Kip Tullet's young brother, had been in a hurry to get back to the ranch to report the meeting between the stranger and Tom Kettle; it was the kind of intelligence that paid off handsomely as far as Colston was concerned. Howard had watched the man head for the livery but he himself had hung back, close to the open window beside the table where the two older men were seated. He didn't hear the whole of the conversation but enough, he hoped, to put him in solid with Colston.

'You sure about that, Howie? He actually offered him the town marshal's job?'

'Came right out with it, said Serenity needed him.'

'I'll be damned. Fanning, you say his name was, Jack Fanning?'

'Was what I was told when I asked around, it's the name Ryan used to spook Chet.'

'Chet knew his name?'

'Was what I heard. He's got himself some other names though.'

'Yes, I know them.' Colston passed the youngster a glass and then poured some whiskey into it from a crystal decanter before refilling his own class. They were in the living room of Broken Bow, all stone and polished wood. Gun racks and wall mounted trophies, deer, elk, mountain lion, Indian blankets and woven floor rugs, leather chairs and carved frame mirrors.

48

Colston had been surprised to open the door and find the young man standing there, hat in hand, keen like a young hunting dog waiting for the gun. It reminded him of himself in earlier years. A good memory. He had even worn his own Colt in the same fashion. Not now though. Other men carried guns for him and if he ever needed to pack, the short-barrelled Smith he favoured would be snug beneath his left arm.

'Rio Jack Fanning, Fanning John, The Undertaker. A has-been Deputy US Marshal whose last job was rousting drunks in Abilene. Oh, I know Jack Fanning but he won't remember me, that's for damn sure.'

'Sir?'

'Long story, son, you did good today though. Ride back to town, here,' Colston pulled a leather wallet from his hip pocket and peeled out ten dollars. 'Keep your ears and eyes open, anything I should know about make sure I do. I'll square it with Tullet, he can find someone else to do your chores. I'll be in town myself later, maybe we'll have a drink together, see what happens.'

★   ★   ★

'Are you the man they call Jack Fanning. The gunfighter?'

Fanning was standing alone at the long bar. Ryan was polishing the empty tables, readying the place for the early evening drinkers eager to wash the dust from their throats and chew the fat before going home to supper. Fanning looked up from his early evening beer. He had decided on just the one before an early night and an early start away from that place the following morning. There was something about Serenity that made the short hairs on his neck stand on end. At first he had thought it the impending range war, then maybe Louise Kettle, the way she looked at him, almost through him, like he wasn't really there. But it was more than that.

It was like a coming storm, as if the thunderheads he had seen gathering that afternoon low over the foothills were about to seek him out; lightning dancing across the purple hills, a promise of rain and hard times. Hard times he wanted no part of.

'Who wants to know?' Fanning asked, an edge to his deep voice, more than a little irritated by now that Ryan had destroyed his anonymity, staring down the tall, thin man with the grey whiskers hanging off the point of a narrow chin. Pale, piercing blue eyes hitting right back at his, bouncing back from the long cracked mirror that ran the length of the bar, holding them, neither man blinking.

Fanning turned away first, bored with it, fixing his attention to the glass of flat beer. Damn Ryan. Five years and a thousand miles away and they had come together in this dusty town, had brought him near to death, to killing a man, to being offered a job he didn't need and probably worst of all,

51

introducing him to a woman he couldn't have.

'Colston, Sam Colston. I own the Broken Bow.'

'I've heard of you already. They say you own the valley.'

'Most of it.'

'The government do not appear to agree with you.'

'The government is a long ways away.'

'It has long arms.'

'Are you one of them long arms, Fanning?'

'Me? No, I'm just passing through.'

'You not taking the badge Tom Kettle offered you?'

Fanning was about to say no, no he wasn't taking it, but something hooked him. The man knew his business and that did not please him. Instead of answering he shrugged noncommittally like the man had asked him the time and he didn't have his watch with him. Let Colston make of it what he would.

'Is that an answer?'

The man was like a sharp stick. 'It's all you get from me. I do take it, Colston, you will be the first to know.'

'I wouldn't take it, Fanning, it's a bad luck badge, been worn by too many dead men.'

'Thanks for the advice, I'll study on it.'

'Then you had best study on it on your long ride to Del Rio.'

'You sure know one hell of a lot about my business,' said Fanning, his voice much softer than before, a little above a whisper, his focused attention seemingly not wavering from the beer glass in front of him.

'We met one time way back and you were a badge then — Witchita I believe.'

'Worn a badge in a lot of places, I have no recollection of you.'

'It is of no importance.' He paused considering his words carefully. 'You nearly did for one of my best riders last night. He says you came at him out of the dark.'

'If he is one of your best you then surely do have a down-at-heel crew and more to the point, you have a liar for an employee.'

'I know it, but he's still one of my riders and Broken Bow takes care of its own.'

'What's your point?'

'How many men can you kill in a day, Fanning?'

'How many men have you got, Mr Colston?'

Fanning smiled the words and straightened from the bar, turning his back on the rancher, walking out into the early evening, nodding to the grey-haired old cripple who dragged a yankee-shot withered leg and lit the oil lamps on Serenity's Main Street.

★   ★   ★

Ryan had caught all or at least most of it. He slipped out back of the bar through the stockroom door leaving it cracked, watching Colston alone in the middle of the saloon, lighting a long cheroot. The man waited a moment, then followed Fanning out onto the empty street and watched the man in black walk to the corner and turn into the Drover's Arms Hotel, never once looking back.

★　★　★

'He said that? That's what he said, Benny, are you sure it's what he said?'

'It's what he said, Tom, he blew him out. Colston was fit to bust — didn't show it though. Just took it, swallowed his spit and watched Fanning walk away.'

'What is it, Dad?' Louise Kettle asked, walking into the room, the large living space above the empty saloon. The two men were sitting on a leather sofa, Kettle sipping coffee, Ryan with his hands clasped behind his head, one leg hooked over the other, relaxed, part of the family.

'Ryan here tells me Colston braced

55

Fanning about the job I offered him although God knows how he got wind of that . . . '

'And?' she asked, patiently.

'And Fanning more or less told him to blow it out of his . . . ' Ryan's voice tailed off, his face reddened. 'I mean he, ah . . . '

The woman smiled at his embarrassment. 'I believe I get the point, Benny, do go on.'

'That's it, Lou. Colston asked him how many men he could kill in a day and Fanning ups and asks him how many does he got? Then he just walks out of there leaving Colston with his thumb stuck where the sun don't shine.'

⋆　⋆　⋆

Fanning looked long and hard at his reflection in the fly and dirt-specked mirror above the jug and basin on the washstand in his hotel room. Forty-four or forty-five years old, he was not sure which, and showing it in the colour of his hair, the lines in his weathered face, the slight thickening of his waist, the set of his shoulders when tired as he was now. Damn Colston, why the hell had he had to chip in his thoughts on whether or not he take the town marshal's badge? He didn't want it, was ready to ride, would be packed by now had it not been for the intervention of the rancher. One thing he could not stand was being told what to do by someone he had no respect or liking for. He washed his face in the cold water, changed his shirt and pulled on a light tan jacket then, seemingly as an afterthought, he pulled the Colt and its tan belt and holster from his warbag and strapped it around his waist, setting the gun's grip forward across his belly just to the left of the silver buckle. He set his hat low and left the room without a backward glance.

He found Tom Kettle sitting alone at one of the tables in the dimly lit, deserted saloon playing solitaire, a mug of coffee in front of him. Benny Ryan was not behind the bar, it was a new man, a squat Mexican with a seemingly permanent white smile stuck on his dark face. Fanning waited while the man drew him a beer, tossed two bits on the bar and walked over to where Kettle was waiting, the cards forgotten.

Fanning didn't wait for an invitation; he pulled back the chair opposite Kettle and sat down. 'You still offering that town job?'

'Until the fall election, yes. Why, have you changed your mind?'

'Let's say someone changed it for me.'

'Sam Colston?' A hint of a smile on the purple lips.

'Anything you don't know, Tom Kettle?' Fanning matched the smile with one of his own.

'I like to know what goes on in my town.'

'Then tell me about it so's we both know.'

'I could tell you but it's better you

ask around, meet people, make up your own mind. My views may be a little coloured by events.'

'I'll need a hundred and twenty a month, free board and grub, free ammunition, one deputy who won't trip over his own feet in the dark and the use of that ugly sorrel horse of yours while I'm on the job. And a buggy for when my backside complains. You up to that?'

'It's a deal, when do you start?'

Fanning got to his feet. 'I think I just did. I'll pick up the badge in the morning and check out the jail and office, say around ten. Goodnight to you, sir.'

4

Louise Kettle

She recognised the horse right away. The big sorrel was loosely tied off to the thin branch of a lone willow, the girth loosened, a holstered gun hanging from the pommel, the silver shield pinned to the dark tan leather just in front of the Colt. Fanning was staring at her from under the brim of his black hat — all that remained of his town clothes. He had changed into worn stovepipe chaps over faded blue denim pants, a washed-out blue shirt and a red and white bandana. He looked bigger out here in the open in range clothes; taller, thicker in the waist, relaxed. Not handsome in any way, but attractive, the wide mouth creasing into a smile, the grey eyes sparkling as she pushed the paint closer to where he stood. He touched the brim of his hat and, reaching out, brushed gently at the damp nostrils of the mare.

'I thought it might be you, watched you from the ridge aways.' His voice, like his touch, was gentle, smoky, different from the way he spoke to her father or Benny or even to her in their company.

'I ride out this way most days.'

'So I heard,' he said.

She let that go. 'Are you looking at the fishing?'

'Studying on it some.'

'It's much better up stream, those small cottonwoods that stand by the big rocks.' She pointed to where a cluster of trees stood motionless in the still afternoon. 'Sheltered there and the water is quite deep, it's where Dad comes mostly. He tells me there are hungry crappies in there, but they are pretty darned smart.' She smiled. 'He doesn't catch too many and I do believe he sleeps a lot of his fishing time away in the shade.'

'Wise old man, your father. Big fish you say?'

'I said, he says there are.' She smiled the words down at him.

'You hungry, Lou? I got some line and a skillet in my saddle bags. And I have determination.' It was his turn to smile.

★　★　★

An hour later they were seated on flat rocks beside a well-used campsite stone built fire, picking white meat off of pan-fried crappies with their fingers. She thought of the previous moments, Fanning the gunfighter, the killer, The Undertaker, Rio Jack Fanning hooting with delight as he landed the first of the two fish, whooping it up, chuckling as he lit the fire. It was hard not to share in his enthusiasm, his boyish thrill at doing just what he had set out to do. Was that to impress her, she wondered? She found that she didn't mind if it was.

The fish finished, he tossed the bones on the fire and listened to them sizzle for a moment before rising, somewhat stiffly she thought, and heading for the creek to wash the pans in sand and water. She joined him and washed her hands in the cold, clear stream. They returned to the fire and leaned back against their saddles, she heard the mare snort but the sorrel was still, head down cropping at the grass, rich in the dappled shade of the willows growing there. The late afternoon air smelled of fire smoke and old bones and far off up stream where the willows thickened she could hear duck coming in for the evening roost, their nattering a welcome sound to the quiet of their little campsite. She glanced across to where Fanning stretched out, hat low over his eyes, his polished, spurless black boots a bit like the man himself, dusty, worn and comfortable in appearance. She wondered if he wanted to talk and if so, what about? There were things she wanted to know about him, truths that did not come from Benny Ryan.

'Are you awake, Jack?' she asked, quietly.

'Yes, but it's not hard to know what your daddy feels about this spot, man could sleep a whole lot out here.'

'Have you really killed a lot of men, Jack?' The question was quietly posed and she was uncertain that he had heard, such was the long silence that followed.

'Is it important to you to know the answer to that, Lou?'

'In a way, I am not sure how but it is.' And that was the truth.

'Would it make a difference if it was one or ten? Five or fifteen? A life is a life.'

'They call you The Undertaker, among other things. It sounds dark, heavy.'

Fanning flipped his hat back on his head, stretched and sat up, drawing his knees under his chin, resting it there for a moment. 'Reputations are important out here, or at least they were. A lawman with a good rep could get away with running a town without ever pulling his piece and busting a cap. Just to know you could do it and do it well was enough to keep most men out of trouble. It would be a foolish man to pull on Jack Fanning was the word, and the word was heeded. For a while it was, anyway.'

'But you did build that reputation with a gun in the first place, I guess.'

'Yes and no. You do a little and folk like Benny Ryan do the rest. You do just enough and they build on it for you. I am good with a Colt, very good in fact, probably one of the best.'

He paused, seemingly thinking about what he had said. It wasn't bragging, more a statement of fact and she took it as such, waiting.

'A dirt water stream over in Nagadoches, wearing a Palos County deputy sheriff's badge, green, my first job, riding down the remnants of Tommy Glide's family, bunch of low-life killers, rustlers and rapists. The old man, two brothers, Abraham and Moses, they seem big on biblical names down Nagadoches way. There was a half-baked uncle who carried a sawn-off greener down his pants leg — they say he even wore it in bed. They were halfway across the creek when I called them out. I had the sun behind me, I must have seemed like the devil himself up there on the high bank, them looking up at me half blinded by the sun. Well, they decided to ride through me anyway and I shot Tommy out of his saddle with my Winchester, working the lever as fast as I could — he drowned in the creek. When the long gun ran dry I shot Uncle Henry off his hull with my Colt before he could loose the shotgun, which, incidentally, went off in his pants as he struggled to get it out and it took his foot off at the ankle. In the confusion Abe and Moses kind of shot each other.' Fanning paused. 'You sure you want to hear stuff like this, Lou?'

She stared back at him wondering if he was making fun of her or making a point about himself. He had a look about him, a slight upward curl to the mouth, a crease to the sides of his grey eyes. 'Yes,' she said, 'I might give you a column in the *Sentinel* — if it is interesting enough, that is.'

Making fun of him now, see how he liked it.

'The newspaper woman today, eh? Fair enough. It was bloody there for a while. Uncle Henry was a mess but alive and the other three bled out so much they turned that creek red. That's when a Benny, not your Benny but someone just like him, came along. A talker, an observer. He took one look, and lit out getting back to town ahead of me. When I packed them four bodies in, Uncle Henry having expired noisily on the trail from loss of blood from his own doing I guess, seeing as my round only creased him, it was all done and dusted. Deputy Fanning had out-gunned the Glide Gang one and all, when the truth of it was I had not killed a single one of them. One drowned, one shot himself and two shot each other. Word spread clear across East Texas and I didn't have to touch my Colt for a year. Just get someone to mention the Glides and my quarry would turn belly up and beg me to bring him in alive.' He smiled broadly at her. 'And that's a true story, Lou.'

She got to her feet, dusted her leather divided riding skirt, bent down, picked up a small stone and threw it at him. Fanning yelled, rolled over and dodged behind a rock.

'I don't like being made fun of, it was a genuine question.' She lobbed another rock, a bigger one this time at him and he ducked back down. She could hear him laughing and it made her smile. 'Oh come on out, I'm not going to hurt you.'

Fanning stood up cautiously; he was very dusty, but smiling. She grinned back at him. 'Was that really a true story?'

'Every word of it, Lou.' He walked towards her, palms opened out towards her. 'I swear to God, that was how it happened, how it started, that's how it always happens. Like I said, you do just enough and someone else will do the rest for you. The Glides did me a favour.' He reached her, and stood in front of her, not smiling now, his hands at his sides, staring at her. 'If it is important to you, I have killed maybe ten men from behind a badge and there was never a single one I did not first give the option to come in clean or pull first. And if this is important to you then listen, I don't want to kill anyone else, but I will honour this badge, and I will use my gun if I have to.' His voice was matter of fact.

Instinctively she reached up and touched his cheek, but before he could move she turned her back and picking up her saddle with the ease of a man, she walked to the mare and swung the leather over the animal's back. She could feel his eyes on her as she set the tack and tightened the girth before hooking her foot in the wooden stirrup and mounting the pony in one easy motion. She reined it away and looked down at him, noting the uncertainty in his expression and liking it that way. 'It was a fine meal, Jack, ask me again sometime.' Then she worked her knees and heels and the excited pinto rushed up the bank and carried her off towards the distant town of Serenity. He watched her out of sight, his view blocked by a bend in the trail and wondered at her being there, thinking maybe her father had put her up to it to find out what he was thinking, maybe even what kind of a man he had put behind the town badge.

★　★　★

There was no question as to where the law stood on the open Belstone County range. The federal government had allocated one hundred and twenty acres to any man, woman or family who worked and proved the land for five years. The ranchers who ran their cattle over that open range were reluctant to see it ploughed or even ranched by an incomer, a squatter, a sodbuster. Early on it had proved a bone of contention from Wyoming to Oklahoma and on down through the rich grasslands of the south west. It was a position that many in Washington had a great deal of sympathy for, after all the ranchers had made the land comparatively safe by killing or driving away the American Indians, bringing a rough and ready law to the countryside. Why should they hand over to a bunch of newcomers? But the Homesteader Act was law and Washington was bound to enforce it. US Marshals were thin on the ground and the cavalry stretched even further in dealing with the disgruntled natives, not happy with being driven from their hunting grounds and were, especially the Apache and the Kiowa, proving to be more than a time-consuming handful elsewhere in the Lone Star State of Texas.

Fanning studied on the badge for a

long while after the dust of Louise Kettle's passing. This was bigger than just a land grab though, there was something more to this and he was not at all sure taking the badge had been the smartest move to make. Sawcross, the town he was headed for, was just a border town job, a town marshal hired by the citizens committee and paid for by them to keep a semblance of law and order, a town a long way from Del Rio and not important enough to warrant an appointed deputy sheriff. What was it Kettle had said about the two dead Serenity lawmen? They were bad luck bound and poor horsemen. Was he hinting at murder, two officers of the law assassinated? He had let it slide but it required further examination.

As darkness fell, he reluctantly packed away his fishing gear and saddled the sorrel, swinging aboard the big yet surprisingly gentle animal and walked it down through the trees, into the scrub and onto the more used trail leading back to town. Without any warning a stiff, cool breeze suddenly sprang up followed by a hard rain as so often happens in the south west. He paused long enough to unwind his yellow slicker from behind the saddle cantle and wrapped it around his shoulders, conscious of the lightning low across the distant foothills followed by the muted boom of thunder and was relieved to see the dim lights of Serenity through the dying misty rain.

*   *   *

Fanning arose early the morning following his encounter with Louise Kettle in the foothills. He had a quick breakfast at the Red River Café noting that Anne, the usual waitress, was not on duty and had been replaced for the morning shift by a limping man with a fixed smile and friendly manner. He ate his three eggs over easy, drank two cups of indifferent Joe and headed for the jail and his morning appointment with a deputy selected for him by

Tom Kettle. He was about to leave when Ryan, the bartender and part owner of the Cattleman's Rest, came through the doorway and made a beeline for Fanning's table.

'Mind if I take a seat?' he asked.

Fanning nodded his head and pushed the chair towards the man with a polished boot. 'Make yourself to home.'

'Tom suggested I show you around town, introduce you to a few of the business men, point out the good and the not so good and maybe fill you in on Serenity's background — like all towns it has a sunny upside during the day and a dark underbelly come dark on payday or any damned day. We've had three shootings here in the last six weeks and I lost me a good bartender last week when there was a ruckus in the Cattleman's and he near as damn it got his head shot off. He up and left the next morning, said he felt safer in Dodge even before Earp cleaned it up.' He grinned. 'That Wyatt was one damned running gun.'

Fanning listened, the man loved to talk and he knew stuff, things no one but a bartender could know and he knew it would be wise to listen and to look where he pointed.

The town was set on a slight rise in the prairie and open to the wind which Fanning thought was fine in the summertime with the cool breeze refreshing the hot and sometimes fetid air of the town, but would not be so comfortable in winter with snow and rain coming down off the distant hills and from the mountains beyond. A full Saddlebrook Creek, a tributary of the far off Serenity River, ran to the south east of the town and there was some sparse woodland to the north else it was mostly mesquite, sage and prairie grass, a rich land offering plenty for both ranchers and farmers and, should they be persuaded to choose the Serenity option, fairly easy grading for the railroad engineers.

Serenity was split in two. To the south of Main Street was what Ryan referred to as the Mexican Quarter with a fair selection of cantinas and whorehouses, mostly drink and very little gambling. To the north of Main Street the business sector with its three saloons; the Cattleman's Rest, The Pink Lady, and Cappy Doolittle's Longhorn Bar and Billiard Hall. There were two general stores, two hotels, a selection of eating houses, a gunsmith's, livery stable, church, town hall, Doc Henderson's place, land-office-cum-assay-office and one substantial bank. The jail and marshal's office were next to the Doolittle's undertaking business and offered limited living accommodation to the badge holder. Most of the businesses had living quarters above them but the main residences were still a little further to the south east, well away from the so-called Mexican Quarter. One thing was clear; there was plenty of room for expansion should the town boom as was likely if the railroad came and that would only happen if the money men felt the town to be safe for its workers and paying passengers.

Ryan introduced him to many of the business owners, who greeted the newcomer with a certain reverence while keeping a wary distance between he and they. Only those directly on the town council showed him any warmth, backed by a friendly handshake. That was to be expected he knew, law tends to quieten a town and could drive away trade. The trick was to be firm and fair and recognize the need for men to let off a little steam without getting their heads busted by an overzealous lawman. This was not Rio Jack Fanning's first rodeo.

5

Aaron Gumm

Aaron Gumm was a lone stone killer. He was not a running gun for hire; he was a skilled and deadly assassin of the highest order. His contracts ordered him to kill, not to wound, not to deter but to kill, to end it there with any given target man or organization. He had a free hand to generate fear and distrust. Death was his calling card; he enjoyed his work. By pistol or knife from a darkened alleyway, from a distance by his beloved Sharps rifle, by his strong, bare, dirty fingernailed hands or simply by improvising, arranging an accident. Wherever and for whatever reason, death was his master and his chosen profession. At night, the dead did not come calling — he sought them out, found them one by one, some more memorable than others. Their dead, startled eyes fodder for his dreams. Aaron Gumm had never had a nightmare, never a bad memory or a night-cold moment in his life. He looked upon it as a calling, a mission, a crusade for God.

A tall man, slight of build with deep-set obsidian black eyes in a skull-like cadaverous face, usually bare of any expression with the one possible exception of when he was hymn-singing or quoting the Bible to himself in his sonorous voice. Sometimes there was a glow of interest, of compassion within the rendition of the words, not that he had any real concept of God or any deity other than perhaps the Devil — and even he would have experienced some discomfort in the presence of Aaron Gumm. Yellow teeth, not through age but through neglect, disease, set in a tight, thin-lipped mouth that exhaled a breath stinking more of stale urine than country air. Dressed in his long, black frock coat, black shirt and woollen trousers, head topped with a low crowned, flat brimmed black hat he could easily have been, and often was, mistaken for a preacher or a man of the cloth in many of the small Texas towns he sometimes frequented. On such occasions he played the role real well, sometimes even leading a little hymn singing, all of the while wondering at the stupidity of people to accept him as a man of God simply because of the clothes he wore. He rarely left the state though and only ventured south of the Rio Grande if his work really necessitated such an arduous trip. For the foreseeable future he was settled, his current contract ongoing. He had requested and been granted full and sole use of an old line shack tucked away in the foothills above Serenity. He had set wires around the cabin with small grenades, homemade from leftover Civil War ordinance, to warn him of any approach be it from man or animal. His employer had also made certain that the place was not to be visited under any circumstances by other employees.

Gumm did not frequent whorehouses, drink alcohol or gamble. When not killing, waiting for word from his employer or planning a kill he sat alone among the rocks in one of his several hideaways playing his harmonica, walking or riding the trails and hidden paths of the woods, singing hymns and talking quietly to himself. He was a very rich man by any standard, with accounts in over a dozen banks south of the Picketwire. He rarely touched the money or gave it any real thought; it was simply there, it was money the weak gave him to do what only the strong could do. Aaron Gumm was an expensive commodity but the rich, the ambitious, could afford to pay for the realization of their crooked grandiose plans best laid in the dark of the night, in still corners and paid for in gold coin. So far on this assignment alone he had in his small strong box, ready for banking when the time was right, over five thousand dollars in gold paid for by the sudden demise of two railroad surveyors and two badges. The latter two he was particularly proud of but unable to comprehend the acceptance of the local populace that two lawmen could die in such similar circumstances over such a short period of time. The weakness in men, the feebleness of their brainpower filled him with disgust and encouraged and justified in some sick way his continuance of a brutal profession.

★　★　★

Texas was hot, baked with summer sunshine, the long grass needing rain was still good grazing for the cattle that wandered the unfenced land and that rain was also needed by the few settlers still trying to prove their one hundred and twenty acres, while looking over their tired shoulders for the threat that had for some time hung over them. So far it had only been a threat but each man and woman in their own turn and in the dark of the night listened for the sound of the hoof beats of nightriders. Such a man was Stephen Monroe, a tall second generation Scot with a strong back and two quarter sections to farm, having taken over his brother's holding while the man was incapacitated with probable consumption.

Monroe sat on the small veranda that gave him shelter from the daytime sun when not working the fields and was taking his pipe, together with a small dram of whiskey, brewed by his neighbour back in the hills from a small but efficient still. All afternoon he had been working on the small barn and lean-to he and his brother had constructed when they had first arrived in Belstone County. With the onset of evening, a chilly breeze swept through the valley and he was glad of the whiskey and the hot bowl of the pipe in his hand as he enjoyed the peace of the evening. Strange though, he thought to himself, it was very quiet; even the small birds that usually dropped by for a late supper were absent, a nearby raptor possibly or they had found better feed elsewhere? He was still thinking on that when the tall, thin man dressed in black emerged from the nearby treeline. The low crowned, flat brimmed hat suggested to Monroe that he was about to entertain one of the occasional wandering preachers so familiar in the sparsely populated farming areas of South Texas. He guessed the visit would cost him a free meal, a sermon perhaps and certainly a hymn or two. He got to his feet and greeted the man, feeling a slight chill at the close-up look of the cadaverous face with its deep, sunken black eyes. 'Evening, preacher,' he greeted the visitor, 'great day but a chill evening coming I'll venture.'

'Evening, pilgrim, yes a cold night ahead of me.'

'I can offer you a hot meal and a couple of blankets in the barn, unless you are heading somewhere else before full dark.'

'No, this is where I am meant to be this night. No food or shelter but I would welcome a glass of cold fresh water.' The voice was sonorous, in keeping with the image Gumm knew he projected and was, as always, so stupidly accepted.

'I can do better than that. How does a cool glass of lemonade sound? My neighbour brings me around a jug of his wife's homemade brew every so often and today is your lucky day.'

But not yours, the thin man thought to himself, watching the burly back of the farmer disappear into the cabin returning moments later with a glass and a large jug of grey clouded water. He set them down on the rough wooded table beside the whiskey bottle and poured a generous glass of lemonade, handing it down to the man, who simply nodded his thanks and drained the glass in a few noisy swallows.

'Thank you, sir, your neighbour's wife makes fine lemonade.'

'She sure enough does and her old

man also makes a fine brew — but I guess you don't want to know about that.' He laughed. 'Sure I cannot get you something else?'

The thin man ignored the question and posed one of his own. 'How long have you lived here?'

'Five years, give or take a month. Two more months and I will have proved the place and it will be mine. God bless the federal government, eh?'

'God bless it indeed but you will not make those two months, I am afraid.'

'Excuse me?'

'You will not make it through another day, Stephen, you are very much in the wrong place at the wrong time and you will be departing this evening.' The man's voice was suddenly very low, the cold words drifting out through the thin lips.

'The hell I will.'

Stephen Monroe was quite suddenly very afraid. His glance wandered across the veranda to where his double-barrelled twelve gauge rested against the rocking chair.

'You would never make it, Stephen, just accept things for what they are.'

The man let the words hang on the air then he reached out above his head for the back of his jacket collar, pulled out a narrow bladed pig sticker and with considerable force threw the knife at the wide-eyed farmer, threw it with such a force that the thin blade sank into the big man's broad chest, only stopping at the guard. Monroe stared down in utter disbelief, raising his head momentarily before falling backwards onto the veranda's wooden floor, knocking over the small table and spilling the lemonade onto the boards.

That look of disbelief, the old man thought, always the same, always that stare into nothing, total incomprehension of what had happened, no idea as to why it had happened, only the darkness and the white face of death.

Gumm mounted the veranda and placing his booted foot onto the farmer's chest, he pulled the knife free.

He wiped the blade on the dead man's dusty vest and marvelled momentarily at the bubbling sound of escaping air from the bloody wound. Then, dragging the rocking chair down into the yard and, careful not to get any blood on his dark clothes, he heaved the fallen man onto it, posing him in a sleeping position. Satisfied, he hunted through the cabin for an accelerant and found a can of coal oil, which he poured liberally over the body before igniting it with a blue-topped match.

Aaron Gumm stood back from the pyre, warming his hands on the heat from the flames before turning and walking back into the darkness of the nighttime woods from whence he had come.

★ ★ ★

Harrison Aymes sat at one end of the long, polished mahogany table that took up most of the available space in the company boardroom. His face was fire red, partly from the half empty brandy bottle, partly due to high blood pressure but mostly due to a frustrating anger. He stared long and hard at the papers in front of him before raising his head and addressing his fellow board members.

'You have all had copies of this document, do you have any immediate thoughts on this matter, gentlemen?' His voice was still hoarse from the haranguing he had given the messenger who had earlier delivered the report into his care.

His question was answered with a painful silence as his fellow board members looked from one to the other, not one of them wishing to open with the wrong words and get a similar tongue lashing.

'Well then, let me tell you what I think. I think we are losing time and money — money we may well not be able to recoup in such a quantity as to make this enterprise as worthwhile as it was when our friend in Texas convinced us to come aboard. I think before we commit fully and further we need to ascertain exactly what the fuck is going on.'

'Just what do you think is going on down there, Harry?' John Wilson Junior was happy to step into the firing line as he was the one who would take over the chair should Harrison Aymes keel over, as it looked like he may well do if he did not calm down, lay off the booze and lose a little weight. Also he was the man, second only to Aymes, with the most cash invested and the fact that cash was not his but that of his father did not come into it.

'I think our friend may have bitten off more than he can chew, which is a mighty big chaw for a Texican, I can assure you of that.'

'How so?'

'We appear to have a lot of dead bodies in and around Serenity which, as you know, would provide the cheapest route to Belstone for the South Texas Railway Company, who themselves seem to be missing a couple of line men.'

'Collateral damage was expected if we wished engineers to choose the Colfax route and not the Serenity River way.'

'True, but how much so-called collateral damage can we sustain before shareholders begin to fidget or before law and order become a priority for those backwoods farmers and towns-folk?'

'Who else other than the two missing South Texas rail men?'

'Current count is as far as I know, two lawmen, both locally employed town marshals not county or federal law enforcement officers, and one farmer burned to death, it would seem only a few months short of proving his homestead.'

'That should put a few of them to the wall, maybe cede their land to our man.' Wilson chuckled.

There was a murmur of agreement from around the big table, a slight relaxing of the tension generated earlier by Aymes, a shifting of chairs on the polished wood floor.

'What about county law, do we have a handle on that?'

'I don't know, it's election year, anything could happen.'

'What has happened so far?'

'No interference, at least not yet, Sheriff Overmeyer wants to be re-elected that's for sure and he needs our support for that, political campaigns are not cheap. However, if pressure mounts he may have to interfere. People of Belstone County are closer to him than we are, money might not be enough. The man has serious political ambitions.'

'Give a man a goddamned badge and he immediately sees himself as governor of the state. Jesus Christ, the man is a moron, he bucks us he's dead in the water every which way.' Wilson's voice was raised a notch.

The mood of the room changed yet again.

'Like I said, John, he's a long way

from here and one way or another, Serenity and its voters are a lot closer. A couple more bodies and someone is likely to holler.'

'That would not be good. If law and order came to Serenity, there is no way that route would not be chosen — it would save thousands and the money we have invested in land around the Colfax area would not be worth a plugged nickel.'

'Has something altered down there of late? I understood a range war was making our investment in Colfax worthwhile.' The dapper Phillip Johnson was the quietest member of the board but when he felt the need to speak, others generally listened.

'Fair question, Phil. Has it changed, Harry? Is there something we do not know?'

'Not that I know for certain, but there is talk of a feisty gunfighter being appointed by the town council as the new marshal. That may have slowed things down some.'

'Do we have a name for this mystery man?'

'Jack Fanning, it says here,' he indicated the sheaf of papers in front of him.

'May I suggest we send a new man of our own down there to report directly back to you? I say this just in case the reports we are getting from on the ground may be biased by greed on the part of our current employee. He stands to lose a great deal if Serenity is chosen and he is not in the position, as we are, to sustain any loss at all.'

'True enough, Phil, he has bought one hell of a lot of land and property in and around Colfax.'

'Harry, I suggest you do what you have to do to make this right.' It was Wilson again, wresting the reins back from Johnson. A game to the young man, the usual boardroom bullshit — it was fun but it was a whole lot of his daddy's money he had invested.

'I'll get onto it right away, gentlemen, and thank you all for your input,'

Aymes said. The sarcasm was not lost on the silent majority of the board members but a head above such a volatile parapet was likely to be a head shot off. What was the loss of a railroad track in the wilds of South Texas more or less to most of them?

6

Moonshine and Murder

It was the start of a hot, sleepy South Texas day. The sun cleared the morning clouds from the sky and then burned the moisture out of the dusty air, making movement undesirable and, for the elderly of Serenity, the breathing difficult. The heat soaked into the more substantial brick-built business premises and bounced off the clapboard buildings, sending a flat wave of dry heat across the empty street. The one-eyed black and white mutt that usually snarled and barked at the loafers propped in their chairs out front of Bert Jenning's barber shop closed his one good eye and pretended they were not there; they could await his pleasure in the cool of the evening. The blue jays that spent the early mornings and late afternoons fighting over nothing in particular settled in unusual harmony in the drooping shady branches of the willow trees that ran the banks of the runoff Saddlebrook Creek to the south east of the town.

It was a hot one and being only the second Friday in June, there was plenty more to come. On this hot day Serenity was aptly named and not at all what Fanning had been led to believe. No gunfights, no hurrahing of the town and not a lot for him to do. Maybe, just maybe his reputation had been and would be enough, exactly as he had tried to explain to Louise Kettle.

In the comparative coolness of his small office, Fanning slipped out of the black vest and undid his string tie. He hung the vest on the back of his chair, after first removing his badge and clipping it alongside of the silver buckle of the shell belt that coiled up on itself on top of the otherwise empty spur-scarred desk in front of him. He settled his elbows on the desk and cupped his unshaved cheeks on the heels of his hands, staring into the middle distance, his pale blue eyes fixed on the dancing motes of dust raised by his earlier movements.

Friday, all day. Unload the mail and the Wells Fargo box if there was one from the noon stage, and maybe wander down for a confab with Tom Kettle. He checked his watch, a little after eleven-thirty. Then maybe dig a few bass out of the creek for his supper, pan fry them in the Kettle kitchen and eat them with Louise for company; she was an accommodating enough woman. Then maybe, shoot some frames with Cappy Doolittle or Tom Kettle in Doolittle's Bar and Billiard Hall, make a change from the usual Cattleman's Rest. Doolittle was a small, neat man with a huge smile and stomach to match. Saturday morning, kick the Friday night drunks loose from the single jail cell and head out to the small two-storey house he had his eye on, take another look at it, maybe lease it or buy it outright with a loan from Kettle's bank. Spend the weekend with the birds and the bees. Walking in tall cotton and better than a long ride to Del Rio and beyond. He could leave the town to his new deputy Horace Jones, a keen young man with little or no experience as a lawman but eager to learn. Enjoy the weekend and pick up the pieces on Monday morning. Not that there would be any pieces to pick up. Serenity was living up to its given name. No sign of the belligerent Broken Bow owner or any of his crew during the past week, maybe it was over but he did not believe that for one minute. How did the old saw go? 'The calm before the storm.' He had broken up the odd drink infected fist fight over a woman or a bad hand of poker, a possible domestic quarrel — best ignored, a badge never was a welcome sight when man and woman were going at it, not even a brawl in the confines of any one of the town's three saloons. If any of the Broken Bow crew were in town they kept their heads well down. The few farmers or settlers that drifted in for supplies and lingered for a drink, a respite from the breaking of the hard and sometimes baked Texas soil, were never any trouble.

Fanning tried to think it through, but the date eluded him. Not Friday the thirteenth, not the end of the month and not a payday Saturday night, he could settle with his weekend and not worry.

Eleven fifty. Fanning groaned his one hundred and twenty-five pounds to his feet, stretched, sighed, ran his fingers through his overly long greying hair and set his black Stetson forward to help his eyes in their battle against the yellow sky. As an afterthought, habit really, he swung his shell belt around his waist and slid the brown leather holster around to its usual comfortable position, pistol butt forward, the leather slanting forward high on his left hip. He opened the desk drawer, took out his firearm, the black handled Colt Army

.45 calibre with the six-inch barrel and the trigger neatly tied back against the rear of the guard with bronze piano wire so that all he had to do on the pull was to work the hammer with his thumb and drop it on the upward movement. He eased the weapon into the oiled holster and seated it snugly on his hip. No need to check the loads or work the hammer; that was part of his waking routine, had been for as long as he cared to remember. Satisfied, he opened the door and stepped outside into the blast of the noonday heat. Pausing, he looked up towards the ridge for the telltale dust bloom that would tell him the overlander was riding the long incline with weary horses, a thirsty driver and a shotgun guard. He caught the wisp of yellow as the stagecoach topped the ridge and started on down. It would be another fifteen minutes; old Moss the driver would not run the horses hard for the last three miles.

In a short week Fanning had settled into an easy routine, shared time with some of the older residents, listened to their yarns, learned a great deal about Serenity, Colfax, Belstone and the rancher Sam Colston. He listened carefully, tried to sort out the chaff from the grain and filed the facts away for any future recall.

'Hot enough for you, Jack?' Cappy Doolittle was on his way to the billiard hall for a midday schooner of beer.

'Too damned hot. I'll check for the payroll and join you for a beer.' He looked up to the rise, his eyes half closed against the glaring sun. There was no dust. 'Damn, old Moss is taking his time.'

Then that odd old feeling, the premonition of the long-time lawman, a tensing of the spine, suddenly becoming aware of the hair on the back of his neck. Trouble. No dust because the stage wasn't moving and there was no reason for it to stop on the long incline, the opposite in fact, a downhill roll, across Serenity Creek and home.

'Cappy, dig my deputy out of the

saloon tell him to saddle the sorrel, find the doc while you are at it and get him over here, pronto.' There was an urgency in his voice that the older man could not deny and he was running across the street to the livery while Fanning stepped back inside his office and unchained a Winchester from the rack, shoved a half dozen shells in the loading port, worked the lever and gently lowered the hammer onto half cock above the live round.

The big sorrel moved easily between his thighs, glad to be out of the gloom of the livery, the trot breaking to a run as they hit the incline. Two miles up, it was a hot ride and within minutes both animal and rider were sweating. Fanning eased the animal in and with the rifle's stock against his thigh turned the last bend in the long slope. The horse slid to a halt and half turned, its eyes wide, snorting its displeasure at the smell of death. Fanning fought him, turned him forward again, talking to the animal, his voice soft. 'Easy, horse, easy.'

The lead horse of the matched four chestnuts was down and dead. It must have died midstride, its legs splayed, the other three horses, one bloody around the neck, bunched up behind it, the coach slewed across the trail. Old Moss's limp, black hand dangled down and out of the deep well beneath the driver's seat. There was no sign of Stevens, the regular shotgun guard.

Fanning looked over the lip of the well. Moss was staring back up at him with wide-open deep brown eyes, but he was looking at another world somewhere far away from Serenity. There was a neat hole in his left temple and a bloody, ragged one in the right, leaking white brain matter and pink fluid. There were powder burns around the entrance wound.

A horse snorted and coughed. Fanning turned his attention to the animals, noting as he did so a cloud of dust coming up the rise. Tom Kettle and half the town he guessed.

The second lead horse was shot through the throat. The animal trembled, stared at him, waiting.

Fanning took out his lock knife and cut the trace and harness before uncoupling the shaft and leading the trembling, staggering animal around the bend of the trail. He pushed it gently to the side of the rocky incline where its body would not block the trail and drew his Colt, cocking it as he did so and capping the round behind the animal's left ear. The horse surged forward and then crumpled beside the rocks, a heavy sigh issuing from the blood frothing around its soft muzzle. Fanning was no great lover of horses but killing one, for any reason, was a hard day's dirty work.

That was it, there were no passengers, no strong box and no shotgun guard although the canvas and leather US Mail Sack was still sealed and intact. Strange, thought Fanning, drawing a conclusion from that small fact but not from the others. The passenger manifest later showed there to be no paying passengers this trip and no Wells Fargo strong box, so that just left the missing guard and his shotgun. He sent Horace Jones and two other riders to spot the back trail for the guard and took the leashes of the two remaining horses and with the sorrel tied off at the boot, he slowly rode the big coach down the incline, across the creek and on to the livery stables for the owner to take care of, his business, the livery acting as a swing station for Overland. Late afternoon the deputy rode back into town on a tired horse, the other two riders doubled up on one animal and the gun guard's body covered with a tarp and across the saddle of the third rider's horse. He had also been shot in the head at close range, the powder burns clearly visible.

Much later that evening and following a meal in the Red River Café, Fanning and Kettle retired to the back room of the Cattleman's advising Benny Ryan that they would like not to be disturbed. Presently they were joined by Louise Kettle, but neither man saw that as an unwanted interruption in their deliberations. Fanning found himself more than a little attracted to the younger woman but carefully kept his own council on that score telling himself that for one thing she was too young for him, she would never feel the same way and, in any case he was possibly still on his way to Del Rio.

'It was not a hold-up in the normal way of things,' Fanning offered, 'and the mail was untouched, suggesting that whoever did the killing did not want any federal interference, as there surely would have been had the mail been interfered with.

'Senseless, a goddamned waste, I've known old Moss going on for over twenty years — never hurt a fly and the young guard was his son-in-law, the wife is visiting her mother in New Orleans. I'll get a wire off to her first thing in the morning, damned shame, what a mess.'

Louise poured them a coffee each and Kettle laced both mugs with a generous slug of bourbon, his favoured drink. 'This doesn't appear to have anything do with a range war, no reason for either the farmers or Colston to be involved.' She refilled her own mug but declined the offered shot of alcohol.

The old man was conscious of the fact that she hovered close to Fanning, her dress brushing against him. It was something else for him to think about.

Nothing much to add to the general speculation, Fanning finished his drink and said his goodnights. Louise followed him to the door and handed him his black Stetson. 'You forgot your hat.'

'Thank you, Lou, it's a damn fine hat isn't it? I bought it in Cheyenne a long time ago, my head wouldn't be the same without it.' He smiled and touched her hand, she did not draw away and Fanning turned and left her standing there, glad that it was dark and she could not see the blush that darkened his lean face.

★ ★ ★

Stretch Hollis carefully filled each of
the four stoneware jugs with moonshine
and gently tapped home the wooded
stoppers with a mallet he had specially
made for the job. After first making sure
the still was hidden by the brush he had
dragged over the entrance to the narrow
gulley, he loaded the precious cargo
onto his buckboard and taking one last
look around, he climbed aboard, kicked
off the brake and drove the pair of
sturdy plough horses out of the scrub
and onto the trail that would take him
to the Perkins' place.

Hollis had his day mapped out
clearly in his head. First call would be
to Heck Perkins where he would get a
look of disapproval from the man's
wife, a dark-faced woman of colour, his
long-suffering partner of thirty years,
and then continue his journey onto Jed
Curry's place. Jed's wife was a little
more hospitable and he would most
likely be invited to a midday meal of

cheese and onions, served with freshly baked bread and all three would sample the brew and, he was sure, approve of its mellow flavour. After the meal, a drink and a pipe he would say his goodbyes until the next run and head out to Stephen Monroe's place. Steve lived alone; a long-time widower he enjoyed company as often as possible. A hospitable man liked by the whole of the homesteading community, but running land a little further down the valley which made for fewer visitors. There he would have supper, probably get drunk and spend the night in the barn under warm blankets and head back to home at first light but not before partaking of an excellent breakfast. Yes, it was going to be one fine day. The sun was shining and by mid-afternoon his day was nearly complete and had panned out just as he had planned it, with one lone difference. That being, for some weird reason he did not want to think about, Perkins' wife had insisted on tasting the alcohol and was singing a discordant version of 'The Yellow Rose of Texas' when he had left and she had even smiled and waved to him. The song had long been a favourite of the Hollis homestead, his daddy having ridden briefly with John Bell Hood's Texas Brigade who had adopted it as their marching tune. Sad to hear it murdered in such a way, but happy to have her give him a smile to remember.

The team broke through the trees that surrounded the Monroe holding and Stretch could see the rocking chair in the yard with its back toward him. Strange he thought, maybe old Steve was working on the veranda, it certainly needed some attention and maybe a lick or two of paint. He pulled the team to a halt as close as possible to the well in order to shorten the distance of toting two full and heavy water buckets for the horses. Jumping down, he called for his friend and when there was no reply he made for the cabin, passing the chair and noticing for the first time that the back was badly burned. That explained why it was away from the cabin but as he walked past, he saw the blackened bundle of what appeared to be burned clothing then, quite suddenly, he realised it was Monroe's body. The cremated cloth and flesh of the man fused to the wood of the rocking chair by what must have been a burst of extreme heat, hot enough to burn the surface of the chair and its contents but not fierce enough to devour the whole thing.

Stretch sat down on the raised floor of the veranda and was sick to his stomach, a great ache, a great loss, no thought of the why or the how of it, only the empty feeling. He returned to the buckboard, hoisted out a jug and took a long, deep swallow. He was a resourceful man, a big man in every way; the moment of regret passed and the need to deal in some way with the situation became apparent. He needed to get the death reported and get the body to Serenity, but how? The remains were stuck fast to the scorched wood and as strong as he was he could not lift it onto the bed of the buckboard. He dragged the remains of the chair and its grisly contents over to the small barn and using the hay hoist and some rope, hauled chair and corpse high enough to move the flatbed underneath before lowering it down again and covering it with a dusty tarpaulin he found in the barn. He went into the cabin and filled a gunny sack with any of the very personal possessions he could find, pocket watch, the deed relevant to the Homestead Act, a sepia photograph of a handsome, buxom lady smiling for the camera and left the place to its ghosts, carefully closing the door behind him. He took one last look around and kicking off the brake, drove out of the yard with the blackened body of the dead farmer sitting upright in the rocking chair covered in a tarp, with his lifelong possessions in a grey gunny sack at his feet. It was going to be a long drive and a sad one for Stretch

Hollis, but he had the jug and the memory of the Perkins woman singing his song, a memory he would have dearly loved to share with Stephen Monroe.

7

Saddlebrook Creek

Doc Henderson worked slowly but he was very efficient for a country doctor, with little experience at conducting post mortems but what knowledge he had, he used well. Kettle stood close to the table but Fanning chose to stay in the doorway. He did not have a stomach for that sort of thing and Monroe's burned remains laying on the doctor's treatment table held no attraction for him whatsoever. Dead was dead. A careless cigarette maybe? Too much home brewed white lightning? Odd though that he was sitting on his rocker way out in the yard but it had been a fortnight of very hot nights and he himself, after a nightcap or two with Cappy or Tom Kettle, had thought how pleasant it would be to sleep under the

Texas stars and wish upon a few of them.

'Gentlemen, I am no expert on such matters but I am a great observer and I can tell you for absolute certainty that our friend here did not die from the fire, he was a dead man when that was lit. His lungs and the inside of his mouth are in no way scorched. And there is the distinctive stink of coal oil on parts of the pants he was wearing and . . . ' He paused, thought about his words very carefully, perhaps too carefully it seemed to Fanning and added, 'I also found a knife wound in his chest so deep that the tip of the blade almost reached his spine. A stabbing or thrust with considerable force behind it — he would have been dead before he hit the ground.'

Suddenly interested in the proceedings, Fanning stepped forward and looked down the blackened body. 'You can tell that from this?'

'The lungs were simple enough to check and once I had found them to be in the condition they were, I looked for other causes, harder to find but there if you looked hard enough. You want me to show you?'

'No, thank you, Doc,' Fanning said, turning to Kettle who also shook his head.

'It was an unusual blade, not a Bowie or a skinning knife, more of a stiletto, a very long, very thin blade, certainly over eight inches long and very pointed. Perhaps a throwing knife? Whatever, I cannot be certain of that, not being an expert on such things.'

'Get Cappy to arrange for his burial. If he didn't have any money the town council will foot the bill and I will send someone out to his cabin for a looksee. Can't ask you to go, Jack, this is county business not the town's concern, then again, if you wanted to . . . ' He let the words hang in the air for a moment, waiting for a reaction.

'I feel like a ride today. I'll get the farmer who brought him in to show me the way if he's still in town.'

'Stretch Hollis, he has a still back in the hills he thinks nobody knows about. Good stuff I hear — make friends with him, get us a jug or two.' Kettle was smiling. So a good man was gone, what the hell — today was a new day, he would be remembered and missed but from what was known of the man he would not want too much wailing above his grave.

'No need for the town to bury him, Tom,' Henderson said. 'He had forty dollars in his poke and a gold pocket watch to boot. Maybe we can drink anything that is left over, as far as I know he had no kin hereabouts, been alone since his wife left him.'

'Thought he was a widower,' Kettle said.

'No, she left him for a cowhand used to ride with Broken Bow two years before Colston bought it, they only worked the homestead together for a couple of months before she upped and ran. He told me that one time while I was setting his broken leg, didn't want anyone else to know. I heard later she was killed by a 'gator somewhere up on the Trinity. Funny old world, it sure enough is.'

★   ★   ★

'You're telling me folk know about my still?' Fanning nodded, sitting on the buckboard bench on a cotton-filled cushion he had borrowed from Louise Kettle before starting on the journey. He had the sorrel tied off behind but had wanted to ride beside the farmer; talking was information and the more he knew about Belstone County, Serenity, Colston and Colfax, he thought the better off he would be.

Earlier that morning Fanning had met with the local land agent at the small two-storey house on the edge of town, on a side street that ran by where Saddlebrook Creek entered the town. It was freshly painted and in good order with a small corral to one side and red barn out back. A small garden behind a picket fence had been well cared for by the previous owners, a lawyer and his wife who had moved back to Dallas as there was no great call for the man's services in Serenity. Fanning liked it right off; maybe plant some roses. He was not happy about living in the back room of the jail house, noisy and not always very sanitary. On impulse he made an offer on the house. It was accepted by the agent subject to mortgage and he reckoned Kettle would spring for that.

Plant some roses? Rio Jack Fanning was going through a difficult time. His whole attitude to life seemed to have changed since meeting with Louise Kettle, not necessarily because she was a good-looking woman, one he suspected was far out of his reach, but because her attitude to life was so cheerfully optimistic. He had arrived in Serenity in the middle of a gunfight, had wanted to be gone and on his way to Del Rio but somehow he was still there. Worse, he was wearing a badge he did not particularly care for and in the middle of trouble the origin or reason for which he did not fully understand. But Louise was the draw. Quite simply he liked being around her but in no way did he think of trying to court her. Still, if Serenity settled down and trouble diverted it would be a fine place to make a final stand. He had made friends, another thing that did not come easily to him, and vaguely wondered about making the town marshal job a permanent venture, even maybe thinking about a county sheriff's badge. He was capable of that and had in fact held such a position in the past.

He was daydreaming and he knew it but she had that effect on him. The buckboard bounce woke him as it jarred to a stop in front of the Monroe homestead. He climbed down, untied his horse and thanking Stretch Hollis for the ride said his goodbye then added, 'Mr Kettle would sure enough like you to drop him by a couple of your jugs next time you are in town, you do that for me and I will not alert the US Marshal's Service as to your activities back there in the cottonwoods.'

If Hollis saw the humour in Fanning's words he did not show it, just shook his head in resignation, waved and steered the big horses into the trees. Fanning watched him out of sight and went into the cabin. Nothing had been disturbed, no signs of a struggle, simply a working man's home with dirty dishes in the sink under a dripping hand pump. Nothing of any value he could see and the only firearm an aging double-barrelled Greener with two unfired hulls in the breech. He removed the cartridges and propped the weapon on the rack he assumed was its home.

The veranda also proved to be barren of signs of any struggle and there were no bloodstains he could find to indicate there had been an altercation inside or outside of the building. Just behind the treeline he found where a horse had been tethered, the ground dented and the grass flattened where the animal had rolled. Droppings indicated it had been a week or so past and may have been at around the time of the killing but that was all. Not an entirely fruitless journey though, as sometimes it is what you do not find at a crime scene is just as valuable as what you do. If the man attached to the horse were the killer he was a non-smoker, no indication of cigarettes hand rolled or tailor made. He would also have been a strong man, certainly strong enough to carry a man's body out to the yard. He was also not of a destructive nature or he would have burned the body on the veranda and cared less about taking the house down with it. Not much to go on, he had to admit, but it was a start. One other small thing he had noticed, the one whiskey glass, one lemonade glass and the broken lemonade bottle. He knew from Hollis that the Scot was a whiskey drinker so the lemonade must have been for a visitor; a visitor who was not inclined to drink alcohol.

A pretty rare phenomenon, he surmised, out here in the Boonies.

Closing the door behind him, Fanning mounted his horse and quit the place where Stephen Monroe had met such a nasty end. He again wondered at his own unexpected interest in the affairs of Belstone County and Serenity in particular.

★   ★   ★

The morning following his trek out to the Monroe place, Fanning dropped by Kettle's store and bought a narrow brimmed straw Stetson, his Boss of the Plains hat proving to be a little heavy in the current heat. It was half a size too small but fitted neatly on the top of his head and was practically weightless. Kettle told him he had to go to Belstone on business for a few days but he could wire him care of the sheriff's office there should it prove necessary. Fanning saw an opportunity to visit with Louise while her father was away and maybe take her to dinner. It was just a thought but to give it some meaning, he called into the newspaper office where she and her father turned out the weekly two-pager *Serenity Sentinel*.

The woman looked up from her desk as he walked in and did not appear to be displeased to see him. 'New hat, Marshal, someone shoot the old one off?'

He was used to her teasing and did not find it too mean spirited. 'Too heavy in this heat. Any big news I am missing?'

'No, just the usual two-pager packed mostly with adverts for things folk already know about and if they don't, then they are usually things they do not want anyway.'

'Doesn't sound very rewarding.'

'Oh, I don't know, we do have the occasional murder you may have noticed and that is being picked up by the Belstone County Echo. I get a few dollars and a by-line for that. Can I get you a coffee? Or do you want to place an advert, sell me a yarn about your gun blazing past, anything like that?'

'I already told you most of it out by the fishing hole.'

'Mind if I write it up like an interview, you drop me few extra notes by when you have time? We will sell a few more that way.'

'Sure, what the hell, I don't mind, nothing there to be ashamed of.'

'That's a deal then. Why not drop by the house this evening, I could do with some company.'

'You sure your dad would be OK with that?'

'Why, what did you have in mind, Jack?'

Suddenly he was out of his depth again, changing the subject. 'Just passing by, thought I'd say hello, I'd best be getting on, I may go fishing, quiet around here. Have a nice day.' Then he was gone outside in the street wondering why he found it so difficult to communicate on any other level with the woman when she was joshing him. He shook his head and thought it actually would be a good day to go fishing.

* * *

Louise Kettle watched the tall man from the window, walking down Main Street in his new hat as if he owned the place; a confident man, a strong man in every way yet seemingly speechless when alone with her. If she wanted him to take notice then she was going to have to do something drastic about it and going fishing might just be the answer. She stripped off her black, ink-stained sleeve protectors and closed the office for the day.

* * *

Fanning took the road to the south of Serenity and followed the creek for three miles upstream to where countless winter melts had rushed down from the high ground, causing a deep hole where the creek turned and again headed east. The current had cut a deep, ideal swimming hole and crappie hideaway. He unsaddled and hobbled off the sorrel in the shade of a bunch of cottonwoods giving the animal room to graze but not to stray, hung his gun belt on a branch and unpacked his fishing gear. Within twenty minutes of casting out his hand held line and jigger he had three good-sized fish flapping on the bank. He carefully threaded them on a keep line and draped them in the cool shallow water, ready for an early supper there by the creek or a later one back in Serenity. Three fish should be enough of an excuse to take Louise up on her invitation to visit the Kettle house and another chance to see her. The sun was high and it was hot; he removed the straw Stetson he had recently purchased at Kettle's store and wiped his brow with a polka dot bandana, looking at the clear cool water, tempted but a little uncertain. He checked the ground around the hole for signs but it was clear it had not been visited recently and as it was midweek, he doubted it would be that day. To hell with it, he thought to himself, stripped off his sticky clothes and took a run at the creek, diving in and swimming out to one of the grey rocks that studded the clear water. It was cold, very cold — taking his breath away but very invigorating. Breathless, he climbed up onto a large boulder and warmed his pale body in the hot sunshine, much in the same way as a nutria might do.

Like all westerners, outdoors men and farmers, he was striped. His forehead to halfway down was three shades paler than his tanned face and neck, his arms to the elbow were of a like colour but the rest of his body rarely saw the sunlight and was very pale by comparison. These things meant little to Fanning but he was aware that the top of his head was getting a tad too hot. He reached into the shallow water behind him and pulled a giant lily pad clear of the bottom and set it atop his long hair. He was sitting like that, water up to his waist, eyes closed, his mind in some distant past when Louise Kettle called to him from the bank, her voice soft and filled with laughter.

'Is this what the town council are paying you for, Marshal Fanning?'

Fanning jerked awake, panicking for the moment and sliding deeper into the water. 'Jesus, you made me jump.'

'Lucky for you I am not one of the badmen around here then.' She was teasing him and they both knew it.

Two could play at that game though. 'It's hot, why don't you join me?'

'I don't swim so well . . . it looks pretty deep to me and besides I'm not really dressed for it.'

'Oh, a town girl then I suppose?'

The woman stared at him, thinking, the smile lighting up her attractive face. She wore the loose-fitting yellow dress he had seen her in that morning. 'OK then, Mr Marshal, if you say so.' As she spoke she shrugged the dress off from her shoulders, stepped out of it, kicked off her sandals, and wearing only a white cotton chemise ran to the water's edge and dived cleanly into the water, making hardly a splash, surfacing and striking out swiftly with even strokes in his direction. Reaching a nearby rock, she settled on its warm surface and laughed at the expression on the face of the perplexed lawman. The chemise was almost transparent and the cold water had hardened her nipples, but if she was aware of these things she gave no indication of it.

'I'm buck naked, young lady — you get back to that bank and toss me some clothes.' The man's voice faltered and he added, 'Please.'

'I can see you are skinny dipping, the water is very clear.'

Fanning slid a little further down the rock until the water reached his armpits and his feet rested on the gravel bottom of the stream.

There is no pleasing this man, Louise

was thinking as she pushed off from her resting place and with three easy strokes was standing in front of him, their toes touching on the bottom. She reached up, put both arms around his neck and pulled his head down to hers, gently brushing his lips and then feeling the response, kissing him hard on the mouth. He pulled away breathless, almost as breathless as when his hot body had first hit the cold water. He could hear a blue jay calling from somewhere and vaguely wondered if the bird was believing what it saw, he certainly was not believing what he felt as he reached out for her, pulled her body to him and kissed her again. He stood back from her, almost floating, watching the smile turn into laughter as she pushed him against the rock and shook water from her long auburn hair like a dog, her whole body behind the movement.

'How old are you, Louise?'

'Thirty-five next Wednesday, buy me a present. How old are you?'

'Forty-five. What would you like?'

'Forty-five,' thinking for a moment. 'That's OK then, if you don't die on me or get yourself shot by some trigger happy gunny we should be pretty happy together for a long spell.'

'Excuse me?'

'We will get married in the fall and live in that house you just bought me for my birthday down on Saddlebrook Creek Road where the creek enters Serenity. It's a nice spot.'

'Married . . . ?'

'Well, of course, married, I would not live with you out of wedlock and now that we have been so intimate in this cold water you have no other choice.' She paused, the smile leaving her face replaced by a sudden look of concern. 'You do not have another choice, do you?'

Fanning only grunted, not quite sure what was happening to him. He wanted a swim, some fishing and a sleep beneath the cottonwoods on a quiet midweek afternoon and now he was not sure what he had gotten in its stead.

'Are you lost for words, Marshal? If I waited for you to make a move on me I would have waited my life away.'

'How did you know about the house on the creek road?'

'Oh my, Jack Fanning, you really do not know very much about women do you?'

No, he thought, he certainly did not but felt he was about to learn a great deal very quickly. 'No, I guess not,' he said quietly, still holding her close, reluctant to let her pull away.

'Let's get you to the bank and under a hat, I have to say with no rudeness whatsoever intended, that lily pad does not suit you one bit.' She laughed again, the tinkle of it almost in harmony with the creek water as it rattled over the stones in the shallow waters of the bank, then she turned and struck out with easy strokes for the distant shore.

Irritated, Fanning grabbed the leaf from his head, tossed it in the water and followed after her, the irritation quickly dissipating as he watched her slim body moving through the clear water.

There was a blanket and a picnic basket set out in the shade and a buggy parked over by his sorrel with the pulling horse tugging grass from a feed sack. They made love on the blanket sheltered by the trees from the hot summer afternoon's sunshine, they got dressed and, happy in each other's silent company, they ate spit-roasted crappies and drank cold lemonade, the bottle cooled by the creek's cold freshwater.

★　★　★

Back in the trees, his yellow teeth bared behind the open lips of a crooked smile, Aaron Gumm watched the lovers until bored with their antics, he turned back to where he had tethered his horse. He would have killed Fanning had the man been alone but he would also have to kill the woman and she was not part of his contract; he had no wish to work outside of that given contract. Two days after doing in the farmer, Gumm had found the note in the hollow tree just beyond the wires of his line shack. It was his employer's way of communicating with him and once they had met and set the drop off it was the only communication they had. A note or money, both in a hollow tree stump; bizarre he thought, but not as bizarre as the notes attached. He had unfolded the latest missive and found simply the name 'Jack Fanning' written there in a strong hand with dark black ink and below the name a large black spot. Gumm was aware of the old sea story, the black spot mark of a dead man; it was one of the few things in his life of late that had amused him.

8

Wild Country

It occurred to Fanning, a bit late in the day he had to admit to himself, that it might be worth half a day trying to backtrack the horse that had been tethered in the woods close by Stephen Monroe's homestead. The day was cooler, laced with a light breeze which rustled the grass and the leaves on the trees. He found the trail again and followed it with difficulty for three miles, losing all sign of it by a dead, lightning-struck oak tree, its bark peeling and insect ridden, offering good forage for the few birds out that morning. The sorrel had been breaking a sturdy and rich-smelling wind all morning and was obviously uncomfortable. Fanning reined the animal in close to the oak and dismounted, aiming to loosen the cinch and to make a note not to allow the animal so much free ranging on the fresh green grass that grew along the Saddlebrook Creek flowing close by the town.

He had no idea that a man's life could turn and be lost or saved by a humble honeybee and it was a certain fact he would never know. Standing by the oak tree resting his back and backside from the irritation of so much time in the saddle of late, not a means of travel he would have normally chosen, he leaned against the tree, experienced one of those lonely cigarette moments and would have been happy to roll a quirly from a sack of Durham, a habit long since quit but one that is never actually left behind.

And that moment is where fate had his life suspended.

Aaron Gumm had been trailing the lawman on and off for two days following the encounter at the creek between his target and the woman. Gumm had thought about that a lot, realising his was a simple life and to try and fathom out the human condition in any meaningful way was a pointless exercise. That the couple seemed to enjoy their godforsaken and dirty union in the open air was even more of a puzzle, but one he could bring to an end with a single light pressure on the front trigger of the Sharps rifle resting across the saddle of his motionless horse. Six hundred yards. He lined the leaf sight with care on the man's back, the triggers were set and he brushed the front trigger at exactly the same moment that a honeybee entered the ear of the big horse and caused it to shiver. The movement was in measureable terms infinitesimal but over a range of six hundred yards it caused the heavy .50 calibre round to shift twelve inches to the right, tearing through the man's white shirt sleeve but only lightly grazing his upper arm before burying itself deeply into the dusty bark of the oak tree, spraying wood chips with its passing.

Fanning was surprisingly fast on his feet for his age and as he dived to the left he turned, pulled and fired three very fast rounds, which although they fell a long way short of his position, unsettled the assassin. Without reloading the big rifle he swung up into the saddle and drove the animal hard and fast across the rocky ground, clearing the small gulley in which he had set up his ambush and making for the open grassland well away from the direction of his shack. He was startled — although he presented no danger, the range being way too far for a handgun — by the fact that the lawman seemed to know exactly from where the shot had originated.

Gumm was irritable, frustrated beyond belief, missing Fanning was the first failure since his early days when he was learning his dark craft. It both irritated and angered him at the same time; it also puzzled him deeply. Why would his God spare Fanning, a dark man in his own right, a killer of men?

The Undertaker was a sobriquet that had to be earned. He was a sordid man, a godless man who cavorted with a naked woman on the banks of a stream in broad daylight for all the world who cared to see. What had caused the horse, normally one hundred per cent reliable, to tremble at that moment? He looked at the darkening sky and the distant lightning marching along the mountains way beyond the foothills that surrounded the valley. Was there a hand raised against him from somewhere far away, for some unfathomable reason? He laughed out loud, relaxed his big frame, his yellow teeth bared and turned the horse back in the direction of the cabin, hoping to reach it before the promised storm and big rain came upon him.

★　★　★

Fanning laid low for an hour, then moving through the wood and out onto

141

the open prairie much as Aaron Gumm was doing in the other direction, he headed back for Serenity. His hand was shaking a little, he needed a drink and, perhaps more than ever, nicotine. The sorrel had been badly spooked by the gunfire and it had taken a while to catch it. He had examined the bullet hole, dug out the heavy lead ball with his clasp knife. He reckoned it to be a .50 calibre round fired from a distance and probably by the action of a Sharps buffalo gun. An odd feeling, knowing you could be shot from long range by a killer, a sniper you could never hear or see.

Back in Serenity, his horse was safely in the stable, left with strict instructions to the youngster on duty to give him extra dry feed, a good grooming and to keep him well away from any greenery. He didn't like to admit it to himself but he was getting quite fond of the big animal. A quick wash in the jail and he made for Cappy Doolittle's Bar and Billiard Hall.

The little owner greeted him with a smile. 'You look about done in, Fanning. Buy you a drink?'

'I am what I look to be and a large one would be the order of the day with a beer chaser and your money behind the bar for another.'

'We agreed to keep you in bullets not booze — still and all, what the heck? Set them up, Jonesy, and the same for me while you are at it.'

John Henry Jones was a big man with a big smile and a giant of a waxed black moustache, curled to perfection at its ends. An itinerant cowboy in his cups one Saturday night had threatened to cut it off and just the threat was enough to enrage the bartender who had dealt with the puncher by jumping over the bar, lifting the man above his head, carrying him out into the street and dumping him full length into the horse trough, telling him if he ever came into the Billiard Hall again he would bite his head off a piece at a time. The cowhand truly believed it and not only did he never visit the bar again, he left town shortly after telling his friends he was leaving for Arizona, just to be on the safe side. It was a story the bartender loved to tell.

Fanning tossed the whiskey down and followed it with the beer chaser, taking its back-up to a corner table with Doolittle close behind him.

'Odd that, nothing much out there, that tree must have been struck five or more years ago, thought it might come good again but it died off bit by bit. A Sharps you say?' Fanning handed him the ball and he nodded his confirmation were it needed. 'Fifty calibre and most likely hand rolled, my store doesn't even stock them now but you could ask around.'

'You know anyone owns one?'

'No, not that I recall seeing. You own one of those old buff guns you probably own a loader. They used to be common enough around here when the big woollies were about but not now, a mite too heavy for a saddle gun.'

144

Doolittle was quiet for a long moment then called to the bartender, 'Hey, Jonesy, that old map under the bar by the safe, dig it out for me will you? And bring the bottle over while you are at, please.'

Doolittle studied the unrolled map carefully, its curly edges held down by the bottle and his refilled beer glass. He traced several imaginary lines along the fading trails, indicating the Monroe homestead, Stretch Hollis' not very secret still and on up to the lower foothills to where a line indicated a very narrow gulley and watercourse. 'There,' he said, quietly stabbing his finger at the paper. 'Just about right there on that stream used to be an old line shack, now part of Broken Bow, then nothing almost clear through to Colfax and Belstone in that direction.'

Fanning studied the map. 'Wild country?'

'Some, but mostly grassland, it was the way we figured the railroad would come in, good gradients, a straight line through to the county seat.'

'And the alternative route?'

'That would be by way of Colfax, longer, steeper and of no real advantage to Belstone.'

'Which route do you think they will go for?'

'I would have said Serenity but with all of the trouble and the killing, the railroad investors back east may well cut their losses and go for the more costly route.'

'You think the troubles may have something to do with influencing that decision and if so, why?'

'Kettle thinks it does but cannot think why or the how of it.'

'Can't see it being Colston as maybe some of it would cut across his land, call in some big money for him.'

'Maybe we are looking at this from the wrong angle. I think I will take a trip out that way tomorrow, maybe spend the night at Monroe's, see what I can see.'

'You do that, Fanning. You be careful,

remember a bullet from a Sharps rifle in the hands of an expert can cover a lot of territory very fast with a great deal of accuracy. They say the man hit by a buff gun at a thousand yards never hears the report before he is a dead man, killed by he knew not what. It's something to think about, you getting to be a married man and all.' There was a wicked glint in Cappy Doolittle's blue eyes as he climbed to his feet and smiled broadly. 'Small town in many ways, Fanning, didn't think that would be a secret for long did you?'

Fanning stood up and glowered down at the short man. 'I didn't know myself until the day before yesterday and I am still not sure I heard right. A man should never go fishing alone, that's for sure.'

'And why would that be, Marshal?'

'He might catch more than he bargained for is all I'm saying.' Then he nodded to Jonesy and walked out into the street and the cool of the evening, wondering if Tom Kettle would come after him with a shotgun if he left town on the run.

★   ★   ★

The sun, when it did break through the morning mist that clung on hard to the low lying land of the Monroe homestead, was going to be warm and would, Fanning knew, get one hell of a lot warmer very quickly so an early start was necessary. He climbed out of the blanket and bedroll he had set on the boarded floor, not caring to sleep in the dead man's double bed, put coffee on the potbellied stove he had kept alight all the chill night and wandered over to the lean-to and fed the sorrel. The big animal shook its head and broke wind loudly, looking pleased with itself at the expression on its owner's face.

'I was just beginning to like you,' Fanning said aloud to the morning. 'You sure enough do not know how to make friends.'

Back inside, Fanning studied the

map Cappy Doolittle had, with some reluctance, loaned him and decided on one wide sweep to encompass the rough position of the line shack and beyond that a portion of the flat grassland between it and Serenity. Flat open plain, tall grass dotted with Indian paint brush and the occasional small stand of mesquite, featureless until he reached the beginnings of the foothills which themselves would quickly change to the rocky countryside and eventually to the rugged granite mountains. The line shack was not at all visible from the game trail he had followed and he stumbled upon it quite by accident. It was sheltered by cottonwoods on three sides and a slight grassy mound from the front. A rough timber building and, like most line shacks, it was a crudely built affair for temporary use only and each new resident would be expected to bring it back to a habitable dwelling and maintain it during his tenure of duty there. No smoke issued from the metal pipe projecting from the side wall and attached to the inevitable potbellied stove on the inside, a feature he knew would be part of any such dwelling. Although there were recent signs of a horse, the animal was not in the small pole corral adjacent to the shack or in the dilapidated lean-to that formed part of it. Satisfied he was alone, he slipped his carbine out from the saddle boot, jacked a shell into the breech and lowering the hammer to half cock, he approached the building on foot. Again, quite by accident, he saw the trip wire and traced it to a small homemade charge buried in the rocks and the long grass. Stepping over that, wondering at the need for it by a line rider, he reached the cabin and gently pushed the unlocked door inwards with his booted foot. The hinges squealed; nothing stirred within but he still rolled back the hammer of the Winchester to full cock; explosives in the line rider's yard were not something to be ignored.

The place stank. It smelled of gun oil, man sweat, musky, bitter and unpleasant and on top of that a hint of sweetness — mesquite maybe? A mixture of smells like no other he could remember and yet there was something vaguely familiar about it. Even so, it was far worse than that blasted out by the sorrel with which he had started his day. He gave the place a cursory search and found nothing of interest, nothing to identify the inhabitant and no Sharps rifle or firearm of any kind. With some considerable relief he stepped back out into the sunlight and closing the door behind him, he walked back to the sorrel carefully stepping over the tripwire, swinging himself into the warm saddle and clearing the rocky area as quickly as was safe for both horse and rider.

Swinging to the west to complete the half circle, he took to the lower grassland and Serenity roughly as the crow flies, a straight line as he supposed the railroad would do if they chose that route instead of the Colfax route, a choice that seemed unlikely given the reputation Serenity was gaining for itself. The thought of that would not leave the lawman. It puzzled him a great deal. A range war that wasn't and two dead deputies, both either accidental or, as he was beginning to suspect, intentional. A dead stagecoach driver and gun guard although the mail sack was not disturbed. The senseless murder of a homesteader and a line rider's shack with explosives planted in the yard. And, a little later that morning he could add one other body to the count.

The sorrel suddenly objected to the path he intended, a well beaten but fresh game trail, possibly a new coyote run but certainly not a trail the big animal between his knees was happy to take and within a few moments, Fanning found the reason for that reluctance. At first it appeared to be little more than a dirty bundle of rags and not, at ground level, worthy of attention but looking down from the added height of the horse he could see white, bleached bones, a skull with traces of hair still attached to the flayed skin, the scattered remains of that which had once been a human being. Dismounting and ground hitching the sorrel some twenty or so yards away, he examined the remains more closely. A grey duster with the stamp of the South Texas Railway on its collar. A wallet containing twenty-five dollars together with an identity card telling him that the one-time owner had been Charles L. Warren of Washington DC. A little way out from the body or what was left of a body, he found a theodolite and other scattered or wind-blown paraphernalia associated with the dead man's profession. Down on one knee he examined the corpse more closely. The spine, part of the rib cage and breast bone were completely shattered and not by coyotes or crows. It was apparent that a round of considerable force had smashed through the dead man's spine and out through his chest, leaving a path of shattered bone in between. A heavy ball? A Sharps perhaps, a .50 calibre slug like the one he had dug out of the shattered oak tree. A coincidence? He thought not. Gathering together what he could of the dead man's possessions, and after driving the spiked stand of the theodolite as hard as he could into the ground by the body as a future marker, he remounted the big horse and headed for Serenity a lot faster than he had intended. As fast as he travelled, the sun was well below the western horizon as he approached the town leaving a green flush on the evening sky, hiding the Texas stars; stars that would later shine out over the quiet land as they did every night.

★ ★ ★

Louise Kettle opened the door and could not hide her pleasure at seeing Rio Jack Fanning standing there, weary and very dusty but smiling. Before he could step through the doorway, she had flung her arms around his neck and ignoring the two-day stubble kissed him hard on the mouth then, stepping back, she said teasingly, 'I thought maybe you had changed your mind and run out on me.'

'Don't think the thought hasn't crossed my mind, young lady.'

'Hey, old timer, not so much of the lady.'

He stepped past her, his arm around her waist, moving into the Kettles' small living room, looking around. 'Your father back yet?' he asked quietly.

'No, why? He won't be back until tomorrow. We could . . . you could stay the night, after all we are engaged, are we not?'

Fanning looked at her long and hard. She was quite lovely in an undainty way. A strong woman with a sense of humour; a sense of being. He was a lucky man and he knew it. 'I'm still thinking on that, I don't actually recall ever asking you to marry me, I just seem to remember you telling me that was so. Is that the way it is supposed to happen or should I go see Lawyer Spengler and get his professional legal advice on this matter? And while I am thinking on that, how about some supper and a drink of the 'shine Stretch Hollis left behind?'

Later that evening, he told her of his two days of riding the countryside, of his discovery of the booby-trapped cabin and of the dead railroad surveyor. She listened intently, sharing the moments and the uncertainties with him, finally saying, 'Dad has mentioned, or rather hinted at his own disquiet regarding the deaths of the two deputies.'

'What was Doc Henderson's conclusion? He is a clever man, I have seen him working a body. He must have had good reason to have certified both as accidental.'

'Yes he did — he had no reason than to think otherwise. They were not cowhands, not born to the saddle but they were both experienced riders, and yet both appeared to have died from falling from the saddle. Brady, the second fatality, had been drinking or at least it appeared so.'

'Appeared so?'

'I remember Doc telling Dad that Deputy Brady stank of booze, and he was a known drinking man sure enough.'

'I'll speak with Henderson tomorrow and get a wire off to the South Texas first thing after that. They have a missing man; you would have thought they would be looking for him. But that's for tomorrow. Right now I need a bath, a shave and you telling me some more about me marrying you. Are you sure your old man won't be back until noon tomorrow?'

'Oh, yes, old timer, I am so absolutely sure.'

★   ★   ★

Doc Henderson had not been a great help, insisting there was little reason to change his original findings but he

157

would go over his notes again just in case and, no, he had not examined Brady's stomach contents for alcohol. The man was a known drinker and there had been no need, the smell of the 'shine was enough and, yes, it was Stretch Hollis' moonshine which had an unmistakable odour to it. Following a fruitless discussion with the doctor, Fanning had gone to the telegraph office and fired off a request to the South Texas asking if they were missing a surveyor and if they were, to get in touch with the marshal's office in Serenity, deliberately leaving the request just a little vague. There was no actual proof other than the business card that the dead man was Charles L. Warren and he did not want to draw any more attention to Serenity at that moment than was absolutely necessary. He joined Louise and Cappy Doolittle at the stage depot and awaited the arrival of the noon coach. They did not have long to wait. With a whoop from the new driver accompanied by the rattle of wheels and harness, the Overlander rolled to a stop.

Hector Ramirez, the new driver, kicked on the brake and swung down, looked straight at Fanning and nodded the OK before opening the door and helping an elderly woman onto the boardwalk, followed by a disgruntled looking Tom Kettle who was known to hate travelling by coach and so longed for the arrival of the railroad. Behind him a slim, dapper man in a chequered town suit. A narrow man, with a thin moustache barely discernible on his upper lip; sharp-eyed, he took the welcoming committee in at a single glance, that glance lingering a little too long for Fanning's liking on Louise. Her father reached her and gave his daughter a hug, then held out his hand to Fanning. 'I hear you asked my daughter to marry you, Marshal.'

Someone in the crowd chuckled. Fanning reddened and felt a little uncomfortable with the attention his private life was attracting, but he went with it anyway. 'Actually, Tom, she asked me and when I said no she threatened me with your shotgun, the one I told you to keep locked up when she was around.'

The crowd enjoyed the banter but their amusement was short lived as Sam Colston and his top-hand Chet Baker elbowed their way through the group. Colston reached out a hand to the stranger. 'Mr Billy May, pleased you could make it to our little town.' The man nodded, shook the outstretched hand and turning, touched the brim of his grey derby to Louise who smiled in return. Without a pause Colston turned his attention directly to Fanning. 'I heard about the sodbuster got himself burned to death, pity it's a county problem else you could have poked your nose in there too. I hear you've been riding my range and asking a lot of damn fool questions. It's not your business, Fanning, not town business at all so keep out of it.'

'Actually, Sam, it is his business,'

Kettle stepped forward and as he spoke he pulled a letter from the inside pocket of his long jacket. 'This is the authority directly from Sheriff Ben Overmeyer for me to appoint a Belstone county deputy to Serenity, the salary for which the town will bear.' He held the letter high. 'And I am happy to tell you that Jack Fanning here has accepted the job as of yesterday.' He turned to Fanning and looked him straight in the eye with the merest hint of a smile on his lips. 'That right, Jack?'

'Dead right, Mayor Kettle.' Fanning's voice was only a little above a whisper. 'Did you bring me the badge that goes with it?'

Kettle fished in his pocket and brought out a silver and gilt star, stepped forward and pinned it on Fanning's vest, shaking his hand. 'I think the Cattleman's Rest can stand everyone a drink.' Then adding with a smile, 'Just the one mind.'

'The hell with this.' It was Baker, red-faced and angry. He pushed his way to the front. 'That badge is mine, promised to me and I aim to have it.'

'Easy, Chet,' Colston reached for the big man's arm but Baker shook it off.

'That skinny old fart is not getting my star.' He looked directly at Fanning, 'Get out of Serenity and take your bitch with you.'

Fanning moved quickly, lithe and easy. He stepped forward and delivered one fast hard blow with the lead-filled leather covered sap he frequently carried with him when on duty, having learned the hard way many years before that a bare knuckled blow could do the hitter as much damage as it did to the victim. He aimed the sap directly at Baker's nose, it broke, shattered and sprayed blood down his shirt front as he fell back, sitting in the dust holding his ruined nose in both hands, weeping in pain. Fanning casually drew his Colt and taking deliberate aim blew the top of the crying man's left ear clean off. Screaming in pain, holding his ear with one hand and his broken nose with the other he stared up at the angry new deputy. Fanning snarled the words down at him, 'Twice you have come up on me and twice I have let you live, you come near me or any of my people again and I will kill you.' He turned to Sam Colston who was staring at his segundo in disbelief. 'Take him out of my sight, Colston, and get yourself there as well.' With that Fanning tipped his hat to newcomer Billy May and taking a trembling Louise gently by the arm, led her away and into the Cattleman's Rest with a silent Tom Kettle and the hushed crowd behind him.

★　★　★

Later that evening when Kettle, more than a little drunk on Hollis's moonshine, had taken himself to bed Louise and Rio Jack Fanning sat alone together in the Kettles' sitting room surrounded by an awkward silence, broken only now and then by the rattle of ice as

Fanning refreshed his drink from Kettle's whiskey bottle. It had been a long day.

Finally Louise broke the silence, her voice almost faraway. 'Did you really have to shoot that man's ear off? I know why you hit him, because of what he called me, but to shoot him like that . . . ' Her voice tailed off, faded almost to a whisper.

'It got his attention,' was all Fanning could think to say.

'It was a cruel thing to do. Are you a cruel man, Jack?' She looked directly at him as she asked the question and he met her solemn gaze head on.

'No, not by nature but I do know my job, I know men, I know good men and I know bad men and I can assure you that Chet Baker is a drunkard and a very bad man who would do you or me a very great harm if he could. I knew that of him the first day I met him in this very saloon and to be absolutely honest with you, Louise, it would have been safer for me and perhaps for both you and your father had my bullet killed him that night. But now I believe there is a force threatening, an even greater evil seeking me out and possibly those close to me.'

'And you know this how?'

'When I arrived here in Serenity I was on my way to a quiet, peaceful job down south to a town called Sawcross, near to Del Rio, a job incidentally that is still open to me and I would be wise to take it but . . . '

She interrupted him. 'Would you take it?'

'That is not the point I am trying to make, Lou. The point is something happened here in the Cattleman's and my reputation had preceded me. An ex lawman, gunfighter, a running gun for hire, a killer of men, The Undertaker. It fits me so well sometimes even I believe it to be so, but it isn't and it is right that you should know about me.' He refilled his glass and stared intently at the rich amber coloured liquid and the melting ice wishing he had a cigarette, smoke to watch rise from a glowing end while he chose his words as carefully as he possibly could. What this woman thought of him at that moment and the moments to follow were of great importance to him.

Louise waited patiently for him to continue.

'I may have been one or even all of those things briefly at one time or another but other times I was a soldier attached to the White House staff, an investigator, a detective if you will, and later the same job with the Pinkerton Detective Agency, in other words I have been around the law a great deal more than your average town marshal or even county sheriff. I know of that which I speak. I believe that Sam Colston is corrupt and works for a corrupt organisation, he is not clever or of the disposition to be behind what is happening here. There is much more to the happenings in and around Serenity than you can imagine and I can only get to the bottom of it if I command their attention, their fear. I do not intend to wind up as another riding accident on Doc Henderson's table. There is an even greater evil here than Colston and it has a bad smell about it. I will do whatever I can to right the wrongs of this place and then, if there is nothing to hold me here, I will ride on to Del Rio — but that will be up to you.'

It was a long speech for the usually taciturn Fanning but it had to be said. He finished his drink, got to his feet and looked down at the crestfallen woman. 'It is what it is, Louise, I will slay this dragon for Serenity but I will do it my way and if that means blowing off an ear here or there, so be it.' He tried a smile but it never reached his grey eyes. Picking up his black hat he walked to the door and quietly let himself out and onto the darkened street. The fluttering light from the oil lamps were fighting a losing battle with darkness and the shadows. He walked slowly; he hoped she would call him back but the distant hooting of an owl was the only sound of the night.

9

Washington DC

Harrison Aymes studied the sheaf of papers in front of him, looking from one to the other and back, checking, reading, digesting. He removed his wire-framed glasses several times and rubbed his eyes with a silk handkerchief, one of a dozen presented to him by his late wife; late in the sense that she was supposed to have been by his side for the meeting that was to follow his perusal of the documents delivered that morning. She would say nothing. That would not be allowed by the gathering but she would observe and tell him of her thoughts later and highlight anything he may have missed. That was their routine and if other board members resented her presence, they were at great pains not to mention the fact.

The large mahogany door to the boardroom opened silently and Thelma Aymes swished in, her dress brushing the floor, and was quickly followed by several of the board members including Phillip Johnson and John Wilson Junior. Both men hid their irritation at her being there but concealed that fact well with a slight bow in her direction, a courtesy she received with a gentle nod, the woman knowing full well of their dislike.

The attendant left the room, closing the door behind him and Harrison Aymes took charge of the meeting with a general greeting and wave of his hand. 'I will not stand on ceremony this afternoon, let's just get down to the business in hand. Any objections?' There were none and he continued, a slight belligerence to his tone brought about by the consumption of a good deal of brandy, downed when first reading of the report. 'This morning I received the first report from our man in Serenity. He is not a very happy man and this is reflected clearly in this document. It would appear that Sam Colston has lost control not only of the situation in general but also control of his own men. An Overland stage has now been attacked and the driver and guard murdered, there has been so much collateral damage that even Sheriff Overmeyer has had to bend to the will of the people of Serenity and appoint an official deputy down there.'

John Wilson Junior interrupted Aymes' flow. 'Can the deputy be bought?'

Irritated by the intrusion but conscious he needed the board and especially Wilson behind him, Aymes replied with a shake of his head. 'No, not in this case, the deputy in question is a man I mentioned at the last meeting, a man named Jack Fanning, a reputable frontier lawman who, I am reliably informed, was at one time close to our esteemed President Ulysses S. Grant. It appears they were in the army together so that is one pot we have no wish to stir in any way that the contents therein can be dumped on our doorsteps. He was also a respected investigator of matters such as this during the reconstruction period, shortly after the war. No, sir, he cannot be bought.'

'But he can be killed?' Wilson again, coldly, no great thought as to the actual meaning of the words. 'Serenity is one hell of a long way from Washington.'

Aymes stared long and hard at the younger man. 'I believe that has been tried on several occasions, three times in Serenity alone and on the last attempt he shot the ear from off the head of his attacker right there in Serenity's Main Street. Perhaps you would like to dress down into western wear, strap on a six-shooter, saddle up and take a crack at him yourself, John.'

A chuckle rippled around the room but Wilson chose not to rise to the bait. There would be another time, there always was.

'What do you suggest, Harry? You set

this deal up, where is it going?' Phillip Johnson, always the voice of reason.

'My initial thinking is to abandon the project, sell the land we have so cheaply acquired in and around Colfax, leave the South Texas Railway Company to build through the Serenity route if they so choose, pocket the money and absorb our losses.'

'Leave Colston to it, but supposing it has already worked?'

'I said that was my initial reaction, but upon thinking the matter through I believe we should simply sit back, do nothing and see what the outcome of Colston's disastrous actions will be. Who knows? Only the railway company at this stage of the game. We lose money if they go via Serenity and we lose money if we abandon the project. We move, we lose for sure, we stay put we may come out on top. Colston can always be taken care of one way or another — don't forget our man Billy May is on the scene.'

Aymes sat back down and waited for

the murmuring to stop.

Johnson was the first on his feet. 'I propose we do nothing, what do you think, John?'

'I agree, to cut and run from just one man would be a costly mistake. Tell May to sort it out, the man is not immortal and if half a dozen men are already dead it seems to me that one more should not take too much of an effort. Colston must have at least one good man down there to have gotten this far. Shoot the ears off of the sonofabitch.'

Aymes looked around the table. 'Any objections if I tell Billy to expedite this matter with some urgency, even if he has to kill the man himself?'

There were no objections and the meeting ended as it had begun, with a group of rich men shuffling from a room in which they had asked that another man they had never met be killed with as much speed as possible, just like closing down another store or factory or removing a tiresome dog that may or may not have crapped on one of their lawns.

Harrison Aymes watched the door close and turned to his wife, the question unasked.

'Sell,' she said quietly. 'Sell everything in and around Colfax and buy anything there is left to buy around Serenity. A small profit is better than a huge loss, sell now while the price is still thought to be good.'

'That's the best thing to do?'

'Were I a betting woman I would lay odds that John Wilson Junior is already thinking the same thing. Phillip, perhaps not but the others will follow Wilson. Get in first, Harry, it's the smart thing to do.'

'OK, I will see to it right away. You think that will end it?'

'No, Harry, one last thing to do, call off the contract — or whatever you men call it — on Jack Fanning, the last thing we need at this moment is for any interference from Pennsylvania Avenue. It is my understanding that he still has friends there.'

* * *

Not many miles away from the meeting brought to a speedy conclusion by Harrison Aymes and in a smaller office, the chairman of the South Texas Railway Company sat alone reading and rereading a telegraph received that morning from the Belstone sheriff's department in Serenity asking if Charles L. Warren was a surveyor for STRC. The worrying thing about that was the fact that Warren was one of two such men the company had lost touch with whilst working that Texas county of Belstone. He framed a reply to that effect and gave it to his secretary for immediate dispatch.

* * *

Fanning ate supper alone in his new house on Saddle-brook Creek Road, washed the food down with hot Joe and cleared away the dishes. He did not mind cooking for pleasure but found little joy in the process when it was a necessity. Outside the rain was falling hard and he could hear the small tributary from Serenity Creek rushing and bubbling past. Texas, one minute a man was praying for rain and the next asking God to turn the damned tap off. He was just about thinking of turning in when there was a loud knock on the front door. He wasn't expecting any visitors having only just moved in; carefully he palmed the little .45 calibre Derringer he sometimes carried in his boot and opened the door. It was Louise Kettle, a very wet Louise Kettle standing there with an oversized yellow mackinaw draped over her head and a canvas bag in her hand. He had not seen her since leaving the Kettle living room two days previously. He quickly pocketed the gun, stepped aside and ushered her inside, taking the slicker from her shoulders and hanging it on a brass hook by the door.

'Hell of a night to be out,' he said

matter-of-factly, trying to hide his pleasure at seeing her there.

'It sure as heck is, Marshal, here.' She reached into the bag and brought out a small posy of Indian paint brush and a bottle of Applejack then, adopting the mythical hillbilly accent so beloved of easterners when aping westerners, she said quietly, 'Here y'ar, darlin', I brung ya these.'

Fanning took the flowers she thrust at him and got right into it matching her country twang with one of his own. 'Right sweet of ya'll, honeybun, won't ya'll come on inside and make yerself to home? I'll git ya'll a plate of grits, sure enough.'

They both laughed and the ice between them was broken.

'I don't have a vase.'

'I will get us one at the store tomorrow, just stand them in a bowl of water for tonight. You do have glasses, I hope.'

'Well . . . ' He hesitated and brought two empty preserve jars from the cupboard and set them on the table.

'Oh my, how very hillbilly.' She opened the Applejack and half filled the glasses, handing one to him and raising the other. 'To us, come rain or come shine.'

Fanning repeated the whispered toast and took a deep draught of the rich amber liquid. 'Sweet Jesus, Jersey Lightning, it has been a long time.'

'This is really by way of an apology, Jack, I should not have turned my back on you for doing what you think best for us, for Serenity, it's just that at times I find Texas and the violence it sometimes generates in men very hard to take.' She settled down in the chair by the open fire he had lit earlier, the rain had brought with it a considerable chill to what should have been a gentle summer evening.

'No apology necessary, Lou, it is where we fit together that is important. Differences can be overcome or agreed upon with time, or not, that is life. Part of sharing a friendship, I guess.'

'You know a great deal about relationships for someone who has so few, Jack.'

'I've had a few, I observe, I learn. How's the paper, busy?' He rapidly changed the subject.

'You want to talk about those relationships, Jack?'

'No.'

'OK then, I'm working on another two-pager, maybe a follow-up on that last interview with our new deputy sheriff, if he was of a mind to do it.'

'I doubt that he would be but I will ask him when I next look in the mirror. But I will have something better than that for you pretty soon now, a story that may well be picked up as far away as Washington, put you and your little paper on the map.'

'And would that story have anything to do with your constant visits to the telegraph office, keeping Earl Harris busy the last couple of days?'

'I am gathering information at present is all.'

'From where?'

'I have friends in high places.'

'Hard to keep a secret like that in this town. Earl Harris is a sweet man but a gabby soul, not too much regarding wires he is not tempted to share.'

'Earl knows his job is on the line, so to speak. He will keep quiet, I told him if anyone heard a word of my private business I would shoot both of his ears off. Seems he was in the crowd when I downed Baker and he went kind of green at the thought. See, girl, it pays to advertise.'

Louise topped up their glasses. 'Can I stay the night? It is raining hard out there and the street is littered with deep puddles, a girl could drown.'

'What would your daddy think about that?'

'The puddles or me drowning?'

'No, I mean you spending the night here.'

'If he gives you any trouble you could always shoot his ears off as well.'

They got to their feet and he held her

close, telling her he wished he had shaved that morning and her telling him it really didn't matter worth a damn.

★ ★ ★

Out in the darkness of the evening, sheltering on the creek bank, his back soaked by the rain water that poured constantly down upon his broad shoulders from the branches of the weeping willow above him, Aaron Gumm watched the embrace and stayed until the interior oil lamps were extinguished.

★ ★ ★

Cappy Doolittle fidgeted with his fingers while Tom Kettle simply stared out of the jail house window, amazed at how quickly Main Street dried out and wondering if the drainage system of gutters and run-offs was worth installing on the three side streets that

182

turned off from Main. Furthermore, he believed that if Fanning arrested a few more Saturday night drunks he could fine them or put them to work for a day and get the job done for nothing. It was worth thinking about.

Fanning said, 'Thanks for coming at short notice, I have something I want to share with you and best I share it with you now, then if I should run into a fifty calibre round from a Sharps my living will not have been in vain.' He chuckled after that remark just to reassure them he was only half joking. It was important that his findings so far be shared with the two most eminent men in the town of Serenity.

'I sent off several wires over the past few days and I have had some replies, not enough to act upon but enough to be certain that one way or another, my suspicions are quite valid.

'For one thing, I am now certain that Sam Colston is engaged in and part of some sort of conspiracy to encourage the South Texas to choose the Colfax route, rather than the obvious least expensive and less time consuming route through Serenity. That can only be because he has a vested interest in Colfax, an interest that is worth more than he would gain should it cross his land whole or in part. I believe our friend Colston is in cahoots with a conglomeration calls itself the Texas Land Investment Company and they, together with Colston, have bought about all the land there is to buy around Colfax stretching from where the Serenity River crosses his land to the outskirts of Belstone itself. Land they have secured without running or incurring the risk of a federal government investigation by the distraction of shining the spotlight on the troubles in and around Serenity. The range war was a bluff, the killings unnecessary.'

Fanning got to his feet and refilled his coffee cup. 'It's hot, if either of you would like a refill.' Both men declined.

'Who gave you this information, Jack,

is it straight?' Kettle looked concerned, grey almost.

'Was I to tell either of you that, I would have to shoot you.' Then adding, seeing that the remark did not raise so much as a smile, 'Yes, it is straight and true. Other bad news is I have heard back from the STRC, Warren was their man and they are also missing another surveyor sent to Belstone to survey and map out the Serenity route. Tomorrow I will ride out to where I found Warren and see if I can locate the other man.'

'What do we do next?'

'I am going to shake Colston's tree and see what falls out — we will do nothing until then. I need to catch the killers, the actual men who pull the triggers, those I can touch but we may need a bigger badge than mine to rope in the money men and I may be able to pull that off as well.'

Kettle got to his feet and Doolittle followed suit. 'Count on me for anything you need that I can give you, Jack.'

Doolittle nodded agreement and added, 'Lovely part of the world, wouldn't want to be living anywhere else, then what? Out of nowhere this shit happens.' He walked to the office door, opened it and stepped out into the street followed closely by Kettle. Fanning watched them go. He had only been in Serenity a short, violent while but he knew exactly what the blue-eyed little man had meant.

10

My Old Kentucky Home

Jack Fanning had no great connection to the Lone Star State of Texas. He had merely been passing through on his way to another place, something he had been doing for the best part of his life. He was born in Western Kentucky, raised in one of its many hollows by his mother's sister, a schoolteacher, after his father was killed in a logging accident and his mother had died of loneliness and a broken heart. When his aunt followed her sister, he was left to fend for himself and he did pretty well at it; he even met and fell in love with Marianna Quilt, a single young girl from the neighbouring hollow. They were both sixteen and more or less alone, she living with Orville, her strange brother, and he with a fleabitten

187

hunting dog he had named Jason after his father.

One sunny, misty morning, Marianna and he were sitting under the shade of a large cottonwood when the pretty young girl asked him if he would object to her kissing him full on the mouth. Jack, a little startled, lacking any experience whatsoever where the female sex was concerned, said no, he would not object, thinking it to be a good idea and an experience worth sharing. They were in the middle of their first embrace when an angry and obscenity-screaming Orville Quilt burst through the Blackhaw scrub, grabbing Jack by the collar and flinging him against the cottonwood tree. The stunned would-be lover watched in disbelief as Orville then ripped a stout branch from the tree and set about beating the love of his young life about the head and back. Size was an issue; Jack was a slightly-built youth and Orville was big, strong and five years older. Picking up a rock as an equaliser, Jack ran forward and bashed the angry man alongside his shaggy head as hard as he could, the blow landing just above the man's ear and felling him like a lightning struck hog. Picking up the girl, Jack carried her back to his cabin, covered her with a blanket and went back for her brother who lay exactly where he had fallen, with his blood-soaked head against a jagged boulder. With a great effort, he half carried and half dragged the dead man to his cabin yard and went in to check on the girl, telling her as gently as he could that Orville was dead and he was dreadfully sorry about that, but what else could he have done?

Marianna Quilt stared at him long and hard, a look of absolute disbelief and hate on her pretty young face and screamed the one question he thought really needed no answer. 'What the hell did you do that for?' Then grabbing a carving knife from the table, she stabbed him in the shoulder and arm before running out through the open doorway and tripping over Orville's still-warm body, falling forward, impaling the sturdy blade in her heart.

It was a long-ago memory, an incident in a place Fanning seldom visited in his waking hours but one that sometimes visited him in the darkness of a hot rain-soaked night. What had triggered the memory that morning as he headed the sorrel across the yellow grassland towards the Broken Bow headquarters, he knew not. Perhaps it was the hint of a past relationship that Louise had queried or perhaps it was something else, the wind in the rafters of his new house, the grumbling of the overfed creek that ran by it or just the fear of a relationship that was going so well at present but which could founder on any stormy time.

Jack had buried the two bodies close together in the yard among the trees out back of his cabin and placed a marker over both and then, standing there, had been at a loss as to what to do next. The hollows were sparsely populated and there was no law as such, but he felt the need to report the incident. He guessed that maybe the hermit preacher who lived in Trencher's Hollow was his best bet. Packing his most treasured possessions into a small bundle, he closed the cabin door for the last time, mounted the big working horse and followed by the hound, he made his way four miles across the wilderness to the hermit's cave situated above a stream that would one day in the distant future run black with pollution from the Kentucky coal mines. The hermit was the nearest thing to a priest or religious elder he had ever heard of living in the hollows. The shaggy-haired, grey-faced man living in a dank, strange-smelling hillside cave welcomed the boy, breaking bread with him and sharing a small glass of the moonshine he had brewed earlier in the week — for medicinal purposes only, he had assured the boy.

'You the man they call The Deacon, sir?'

'I am, boy, I serve the good Lord, this

hollow is my ministry. I listen to the troubled souls hereabouts, I heal the sick, I do His work.'

The man lit some home-made, strongly perfumed sticks from a guttering candle and placed them in a clay bowl, deadening the smell of a long unwashed body and dead animal hides and listened intently to Jack's story, smiling sadly but saying nothing for a long while.

'Human relationships are barely fathomable, boy, the human condition is something I gave up trying to understand years ago. You help a sick dog and if it bites you, you kick it. You help a fellow man and they bite you, then you just simply walk away, nothing else you can do — although I do suspect there was more to Orville's anger than you sparking his sister. Hollow folk can be strangely possessive at times — they will give with one hand and take away with two. Not an easy thing to think about in the heat of any moment. One minute folk like you, love you and even respect you and the next they are reaching for the tar and feathers.' He looked off into the middle distance, dwelling momentarily on some bad experience.

'Do I just leave them there, sir?'

'Buried out back of your cabin, you say?'

'Yes, sir.'

'You mark their graves?'

'Yes, sir, two wooden crosses made out of hickory sticks and string. I put some coneflowers on Marianna's grave.'

'Why two graves? Seems to me they was so close in life, one grave would have done for the two of them in death.'

'It seemed the right thing to do at the time.'

'At the time . . . These things always do at the time, like taking a rock to Orville and Orville taking a switch to Marianna seemed right at the time.'

'It was more than a switch, sir, would have like to have killed her.'

'Them knife wounds deep, they look pretty bad, going to leave scars for you to remember this day.'

'Not bad enough so's they cripple me.'

'You going back to the cabin, boy?'

'No, sir, never going back there, not ever.'

'Tell you what I will do, son, I will go over there in a couple of days and say a few of the Lord's kind words over them and drape a yellow swatch over the crosses, telling any nosy folk passing by that the fever was there. Can I help myself to anything in the cabin might be of use to a man of my calling?'

'Anything you want, burn it to the ground as far as I am concerned.'

Jack wandered out into the fresh air.

'That would be a waste, boy, someone will find it and use it. Where you heading for?'

'I hadn't thought much about it really but I might head up north and join the army. You want the dog?'

'Sure, I'll have him, always wanted a dog. Does he bite?'

'No, sir, and he hunts well, name's

Jason, I called him that after my daddy.'

'A fine name. Now you head north and may the Lord watch over you for all of your days and, take my advice for what it's worth, stay away from women. Oh, and rub some of this salve on those cuts, heal them in no time.' He handed Jack a jar of green cream and nodding, disappeared back into the cave followed by the dog.

★   ★   ★

Five days later young Jack Fanning had crossed the Ohio River, headed on up north for two weeks then broke, sad and hungry he sold the horse, enlisted in the US Army at the Springfield Recruiting Office and was assigned to Fort Yamhill in Oregon where, because of his knowledge of the outdoors, his woodcraft skills and hunting ability he was used mostly as a scout and gatherer of fresh meat and found it to be an easy and enjoyable way of life. Not long after joining though, the War Between the

States erupted around him and the army changed almost in mid stride. The cheerful banter ended; many soldiers, southerners by birth, found themselves to be on the wrong side and dumping their uniforms, headed south. The easy life became an easy death as men were killed in battle or shot for desertion. The Blue and the Grey. Jack had no idea what the war was about or which side he should have been on, but he was wearing the blue and, right or wrong, his allegiance was to the Union Army.

Constantly reassigned, he eventually won his spurs and a promotion at the Battle of Shiloh when, being outflanked by a cannon emplacement on the eastern side of the so-called Hornet's Nest, a young lieutenant was given the task of ridding the hillside of three batteries. The officer, only a year or so older than Jack, had selected a squad of twenty men and mounted at their head, he had led the foot soldiers in a foolish charge at the first battery, capturing it, destroying the single cannon but losing his own life in the hand-to-hand fighting along with six of the soldiers who followed him. Confused, the men looked to one another for a leader and Jack had taken up the fallen officer's mount. Sabre in hand, he led the charge upon the second of the three cannon, routing the gunners but losing three more troopers in the bloody action. The remaining soldiers showed a considerable reluctance to take on the third cannon and Jack, knowing not what else to do, had charged the emplacement on a wounded horse and carrying the officer's retrieved, fully-loaded Remington revolver, he killed two rebels and watched as the remainder skedaddled from the mad boy waving a now empty gun in his hand. He found a canister of black powder in the emplacement and shoved it beneath the big gun before retiring a hundred yards and with a captured musket, had fired at the barrel. The cannon shot fifty feet into the air, raining dirt and bits of body around him and the remainder of the squad. 'We sure did that about right,' he remembered telling them, before remounting the horse and vanishing back into the confusion of his own lines.

As in all wars there are stories, some real, some imagined, of extraordinary deeds and it was so with the story of the Kentucky boy who charged the Confederate cannon on a wounded horse carrying only a pistol. The story spread and eventually reached the ears of General Ulysses S. Grant himself who upon verification of the action interviewed the lad, gave him a battlefield commission of second lieutenant and appointed him to his own staff. The war was bloody and the Federals were finding the Confederates well led and a fighting force to be reckoned with, not at all what was expected. The North was dearly in need of heroes, not only for the morale of the soldiers in the field but also for the public and politicians. Grant had a great need of such men, even if they were only boys who lied about their age.

Second Lieutenant Jack Fanning had served well under Grant and was greatly favoured by the general. It was a service that continued to the end of the hostilities at Appomattox and on into the White House. Not liking city life, Jack had resigned his commission and headed west to become the lawman, Rio Jack Fanning, The Undertaker. It was not a past he would ever readily discuss with anyone other than his own self.

11

Billy May

Cresting a small rise and looking down on Broken Bow, Fanning shook the distant memory from his head, wondering if it would be worth relating to Louise or best forgotten until the next time it emerged from the darkness of the past. So thinking, he pulled the animal's head to the right and rode until he crossed the trail which led straight to the front yard of the large single-storey ranch house.

Sam Colston was sitting on the front porch with a newspaper on his lap and a glass of whiskey on the small table beside him. Chet Baker, his face swathed in bandages painfully administered by Doc Henderson, glared at him while the newcomer Billy May leaned against a veranda, upright. The man had changed out of his chequered tan suit into shotgun chaps over blue jeans and swapped his chequered vest and tie for a faded red shirt and black bandana. He had a Colt Frontier on his left hip with the butt pointed forward, much as Fanning wore his own weapon but maybe just a tad lower than his, he thought. He said to Colston by way of a greeting, 'Nice day, warm but no rain before noon as far as I can tell.'

'You rode four miles out here just to give me a weather report, you must surely love wearing your backside out on a saddle, Fanning.' It wasn't a question.

'No, sir, as a matter of fact I do not like horse-riding one little bit and I often do wonder why God created the horse in the first place.'

'Did you ever reach a conclusion on that matter, Rio John?' Billy May asked, a smile on his handsome young face.

'I have not been called by that name for a long time, Mr May, late of Lordsburg if I have heard correctly and yes I did. I think it was. His way of punishing black-hearted young cow-boys from enjoying life to the full.'

Baker snorted through his bandages and got to his feet; Colston told him to sit back down and turned again to Fanning. 'OK, marshal or deputy, or whatever you are calling yourself today, you delivered the weather report, made bosom buddies with Billy May here and now I would respect-fully suggest you get the hell out of my backyard.'

'Right neighbourly of you, Mr Colston, but I do have to confess it is not only a weather report I wished to deliver, no sir, I would also like to tell you that I do believe the folk in Washington are not at all happy with your heavy-handed endeavour to keep the railroad out of Serenity and into Colfax. No sir, not happy at all.'

'What the devil are you talking about, Fanning?' said Colston, angry and on his feet.

'Well if you don't know what I am

talking about then I am at a loss to explain it to you. Maybe Billy May there can fill you in as to how you fouled the line between here and Washington DC and how he has been sent out here to clear up your mess.' The big sorrel fidgeted between his knees, wanting water he guessed.

'Mind if I water my horse before I leave?' Adding, 'Baker, your hand gets any nearer to that sidearm and I will take off your other ear.' Baker froze as Fanning turned the animal's head toward the water trough, allowing it a few gulps of water before reining it in, turning it back toward the house, touching his hat to Colston, nodding to May and smiling a cold and deadly smile at Chet Baker before riding back the way he had come leaving, he hoped, considerable confusion in his wake. Not long after his departure a Broken Bow rider brought an urgent wire for Billy May.

★ ★ ★

Louise settled in the rocking chair and worked the treadle of the sewing machine, running red thread along the edge of the blue calico forming the cover for the cushions she had already prepared. Beside her chair were a neatly folded pile of curtains she had made earlier for the large windows of the house on Saddlebrook Creek Road. She would need Fanning's help in putting those in place and maybe they could do it that evening when he returned. Curtains were needed; she was a private person and did not like the idea of passers-by being able to look in, also the darkness beyond the unlit street was not welcoming. She wondered absently as she worked the treadle if her father could not bring some pressure to bear on the town council and have oil lamps fitted as in Serenity's Main Street, no point in having a father for mayor if he could not exert a little pressure in the right direction for his own personal pleasure. She knew however that he would not be thrilled at the request and would make all kinds of excuses before acquiescing to his daughter's needs. Putting the sewing to one side and feeling the urge for a cold glass of lemonade, she made her way to the kitchen and reached for the pump handle above the sink, her arm freezing midway as her attention was directed to the appearance of the big man standing by the gate of the picket fence. Darkly clad, a stranger to her, an itinerant preacher perhaps, he certainly looked the part. She opened the side door and stepped outside into the last of the early evening light. 'Can I be of help to you, sir?' She had the strange feeling that the man had been standing there for some time.

He did not answer immediately but touched the brim of his low-crowned black hat and smiled. His teeth were a curious yellow, he was unshaven and she could not help but recoil at the stink of the man as she approached him.

If he noticed her distaste he did not

show it. 'Just passing by, ma'am, could not help but notice your lovely garden, the young rose bushes are a real treat, well planted and cared for.'

'My husband planted them just this week, they are young now but given time they will mature and make a fine display.' Then adding almost as an afterthought, 'He is the Sheriff of Serenity, he will be home shortly if you have business with him.'

'I know who he is, we are old friends and yes, I do have business with him but that can wait for another day.'

There was a hint of menace in the words, almost a hidden threat that did not escape her. 'Well, sir, if that is all I must be getting on with my work, good morning to you.'

She had turned and had almost reached the door when the man whispered, 'You going skinny dipping in the creek again any time soon?'

Louise swung back, an angry, frightened response on her lips but the man was gone, vanishing like a mist into the willows that ran the length of Saddle-brook Creek.

* * *

Billy May looked good on a horse; almost as tall as Fanning, riding easily, reining the animal in outside of the Marshal's Office, dismounting in one fluid motion and tying it off at the hitching rail. He stepped into the gloom and leaning back against the door frame, nodded to Fanning who had watched his approach wondering why the visit, but waiting patiently for the young man to speak.

'Morning, Jack. You surely stuck it to Sam Colston yesterday, man threw a blue fit when you were out of earshot — although I do say he had no trouble restraining friend Baker, who pretended to want to tan your hide but was delighted to be told not to, at least not there and then, face to face.' He grinned the boyish, white-toothed easy smile he had given Fanning when he had first arrived in Serenity, dressed in the uncomfortable-looking tan suit. 'He sure enough values that other ear, but he will come after you, a man like that never lets go. It would have been better for you as I hear it, had you killed him first time around.'

'I tried but he was lucky, a borrowed gun, it pulled to the left. There something I can do for you, Billy May?'

'You know me . . . we ever met? I don't think so. I would remember meeting the great Rio Jack Fanning.' He answered his own question.

'Not as far as I know, we have never crossed trails but I have heard tell of you on some dark road or around some camp fire from time to time.'

'Good things, I hope.'

'As good as can be for a hired gun, although you are no back shooter as I hear tell. A killer nevertheless.'

'One man's killer is another man's lawman out here, Jack, you know that. As long as I am talked about, I am happy with that. You take the badge but

I will take the dollar every time, same job though in the end.'

'That is a point of view I guess, some men are easy to please.'

'Well, I hope you are.'

'And that would be why?'

'Colston has his marching orders, whatever scheme he was running for big business back east is done and I guess so is he, financially that is. None of my concern, though. You are no longer a problem to my employers and I do not have to kill you. In fact I have been expressly forbidden to kill you, it seems you have friends in low places.'

'Good to know. You think you could have?'

'What?'

'Taken me.'

'I am very fast.'

'So I heard tell but, son, on your best day you would not have been fast enough.'

Billy May laughed and got to his feet. 'I am kind of happy not to have to find out if that is true or not but maybe another day — who knows what the future holds for any of us.' It was a statement not a question.

'There is always another day, Billy.'

'One other thing though, Rio John, I am standing down but there is another, a man we cannot inform as to the cessation of the need to eradicate you. A man who kills from cover, a man who will not meet you on the street but will kill you from afar and may even do harm to those you care for.'

Fanning got to his feet. 'This man have a name?'

'Aaron Gumm, I believe, a Kentucky hillbilly. They say he smells almost as bad as he looks but should you run into him, beware not to be fooled by the frock coat, the man is not a man of God.'

'Thanks for the warning, Billy May.'

'You are very welcome, compadre.' And he was gone, leading the horse, moving easily up Main Street toward the stage depot.

Fanning watched the young man out

of view, thinking about Aaron Gumm and paying another visit to the line shack, then turning his mind to the morning's business.

First order of the morning was a haircut, being fed up with Louise telling him it would take years off him. Then pack some grub and head out to the area in which he had found the South Texas Railway surveyor's remains.

Fanning sat in Bert Jennings' barbershop chair and listened to the old man's rambling conversation, wondering if he had any idea of what he was talking about. Like all barbers, he found it necessary to fill any form of silence between himself and a customer with mindless chatter. Fanning had learned as a lawman that the meaningless chatter sometimes carried buried within it useful information, but from Jennings nothing of interest emerged unless he wanted to know the price of a coffin or burial which was a sideline for him and, although he did not display a shingle to that effect, he was keen to let folk know that Cappy Doolittle was not the only game in town if you were dead. Also getting that fact to a lawman of Fanning's reputation could be good for business. Fanning listened in silence as the scissors sheared the long hair, leaving the close-cropped pepper and salt remainder as per the instructions Louise had given him that morning.

* * *

Knowing what he was looking for made Fanning's unpleasant chore a whole lot easier. Somewhere, he guessed on a line to the east of where he found Warren's scattered remains, he would be likely to run across the body of the other missing South Texas surveyor. It was a good guess and a little before noon he stumbled upon a body he identified via the man's billfold as one Gerald Cooper of Houston, Texas. As with his colleague's corpse, the remains were scattered by wild animals and pretty well picked clean by crows. The man had been shot to death by what appeared to have been a big bore rifle but the bullet had passed clean through the body, leaving only the shattered bones to suggest that to be the case.

Fanning gathered together all of the personal effects he could find and as he had done for the other unfortunate victim, he stuck the theodolite into the soft earth for Doolittle or maybe Jennings to find and return them to Serenity for a Christian burial.

He checked the position of the sun; it was already dipping down across a clear blue sky toward the western horizon. The air was cooling and he debated with himself and the sorrel as to whether or not it would be better to pause under a cottonwood tree and take on some grub and a quick nap, or ditch the sandwiches Anne Doolittle had made for him at the Red River Café and head home to Louise and a cooked supper. It wasn't too much of a debate and he turned the animal's head toward Serenity, easing it into a trot.

'Some haircut, Jennings charge you double?'

It was a greeting he expected; he smiled and let it go by him. Why was it women ask you to do something and when having done it, they question the validity of the decision? As at the swimming hole, he knew he had a lot to learn about the opposite sex and he had left it a bit late in life to do so.

They ate supper and he was pleased with his choice of giving the cotton-wood tree and the sandwiches a miss. The stable boy was pleased with the grub and promised to give the big horse an extra rub down and maybe dress the leathers with oil as they appeared pretty dry to him. Fanning ruffled the boy's hair and gave him two bits and a smile of appreciation.

Supper over and the dishes done, a chore he offered to do but one which was politely declined following the breaking of one of her favourite plates when his first offer of help had been accepted. Something to make a note of, he mused. He sat in the leather chair and picked up the book he had been reading on forensic medicine, loaned him by Doc Henderson. It was something he had been interested in when working for the Pinkerton Agency but pounding a saddle with your backside and a six-gun on your hip had taken precedent over in-depth investigations. He would get Henderson to check out the bodies or what was left of them when they were brought in by Jennings at Cappy Doolittle's recommendation; not, Fanning thought, out of generosity to his competition but more out of the fact that it would be a day-long chore and very likely a hot one at that. Doolittle would live to regret that decision at a later date when Jennings informed him of the generosity of the STR in appreciation of his efforts and for the decent burial of yet another of its employees.

Henderson had also shared his

thoughts on the two dead lawmen. Joe Rivers had fallen from his horse whilst intoxicated, or maybe not. He stank of booze on the outside and was known to be a drinking man. His successor Bobby Olds was thrown from his horse and suffered a broken neck. They were the facts, but a strange coincidence. The wound on Rivers' head could have been caused by a fall sure enough, but on checking with the stable he found that the horse Olds had hired was a surefooted animal and had given many years of service without putting a foot wrong — in fact it was a favoured mount of the town's riding ladies. Henderson decided that a conclusion may have been jumped at and both deaths could well have been murders dressed up to appear as accidents. He added that he was just a country doctor and had called it as he saw it at the time but maybe, just maybe, given Fanning's misgivings, he was wrong.

It was something to think on.

Louise handed him a glass of

whiskey, jingling with ice from the cold box in the cellar larder. She was quiet, introspective, not her usual bubbling self. No real enquiry into his day or as to what he had found beyond his simple and brief explanation of his ride out into the prairie. The levity of her opening remark regarding his haircut was the only banter she offered. He waited; it would come without his prompting; he knew that much already about Louise, if not about women in general.

He slipped a bookmark between the pages and looked over at her, smiling. 'Been a long day, Lou, my backside hurts something mean. That sorrel is an easy ride but the saddle is like a rock, I may check out an older used one from the livery in the morning, that or one of your new cushions, which are very pretty by the way.' Adding, 'Are you staying the night or is Tom expecting you home?'

It was her habit to share herself between her father's house and the new home on Saddlebrook Creek Road. Tongues wagged but the Kettles were highly respected in Serenity and Fanning was just about everyone's friend. In any event, folk were aware that he would not take kindly to any disrespect shown either to himself or to Louise and her father. And he did carry a gun, which had become a bit of a novelty in Serenity of late, following his posting of an ordnance declaring that sidearms were not to be worn within the town limits.

'You had a visitor today.'

Fanning was aware of the change in tone of her voice, a concern perhaps, or an unasked question. He waited.

'Said he had business with you but it would wait. He was an ugly man, dressed like a preacher but he stank real bad. Face like an old skull, yellow teeth. Do you know such a man?'

'I may do, may have done . . . Did he say anything else, give you a clue as to the business he has with me?'

'No, but his tone was threatening,

not outright, but hinted at.'

'That all of it?'

'No, I think he has been spying on us.'

'What makes you think that, Lou?'

'He asked me had we been skinny dipping in the creek again, or words to that effect.'

Her eyes were moist, her hands began to tremble and Fanning was at a loss. He got to his feet and reached out for her, wrapped her in his arms and held her, knowing that she had lived with this fear all through the long day, waiting for him to return home to share it with him and then, feeding him, seeing to his comfort whilst inside a wretched, unspoken fear grew and blossomed. She slept close to Fanning that night, very close and he awoke several times before the dawn to find her standing, staring out of the window and into the darkness beyond toward the fast-flowing Saddlebrook Creek.

★　★　★

219

Tom Kettle was just leaving the Cattleman's Rest as Fanning and a pale Louise arrived. She hugged her father, kissed Fanning lightly on the cheek and vanished inside to a warm greeting from Benny Ryan.

'Trouble?' Kettle asked, concern in his soft voice.

'Nothing for you to worry about, Tom, and nothing I cannot handle.'

The old man looked relieved. 'That's good then, I was just on my way down to your office, you are later than usual.'

'Had a few things to take care of. Something I can do for you? I am in kind of a hurry this morning and I can save you the journey.'

'Your boss, Sheriff Overmeyer is coming in on the nooner with the county attorney, Jared T. Parsons. I would like you to meet them both.'

'Sorry, Tom, I will be out of town for a while, maybe a few days. Just keep Louise close by you, give her room, do not crowd but be sure Ryan or you are close by at all times. Wouldn't hurt any if you were both packing a hideaway.'

'What the hell's going on, Jack?' The voice was raised slightly, a pinch of worry around his lips. The man thinking something different about Fanning, the usual blue-grey eyes were startlingly green, angry-looking, changed the way a cat can change the purring eyes to the spitting green of anger in a heartbeat.

'I'll handle it my way, just do as I ask and keep an eye on your daughter and another on any strangers in town, especially if he looks like a preacher. Tell Ryan.' He turned to walk away and then remembered his duties as the designated lawman of Serenity. 'What does Overmeyer want? My guess is he did not come all of the way out here to meet me.'

'We are going out to talk with Sam Colston. Hear him out. We are thinking there is not any way we can prove he had anything to do with the killings, probably the work of some running gun he hired. Maybe see if Parsons can indict him on any of it. Failing that, to let him know that it is over, the South Texas have been informed, information from the east as I understand, that the route will come through Serenity and it would be best for him to sell up and move on.'

'You think he will?'

'I wouldn't budge were I him. Sure he could sell his land to the railroad and run but I don't believe he will, maybe he can make some reparation to those his actions have harmed but that will be it unless Parsons thinks he can prove he ordered the killings and that is not likely. Either way, as a power base Broken Bow is finished.'

'I would like to have been there to see that.' Then adding, 'Horace will mind the store for a couple of days and if Overmeyer wants me to keep the badge until the election, I'm OK with that.'

'With Serenity a railhead? Hell, you will be needed around here more than ever.' The voice was suddenly enthused. 'Maybe you should run for county sheriff yourself.'

'Or maybe run for the mayor's office,' the hint of a smile on the lawman's weathered face, then he was heading for Cappy Doolittle's store for supplies and on to the livery to pick up the sorrel.

'You would have my vote on either,' Kettle called to his back, but Fanning did not turn around.

'Jennings went out after those two surveyors this morning, I'm going fishing, the mayor has visitors so I'm closing the bar. You want to come fishing?' Doolittle asked by way of a greeting.

'Not this day, Cappy, I got chores of my own.' He slapped a list on the counter. 'Fill that for me will you, in a gunny sack? Just enough for a couple of days and add a box of .30-30 shells, a small bottle of bust-head and a sack of makings.'

'You don't smoke.'

'I used to one time a long time ago and I feel the need to again . . . just do it, will you? Bill the office and send the supplies over to the livery as quick as you can, Cappy, I am in a mite of a hurry this morning.'

'You going hunting, Jack?'

'In a way, yes I am, looking for God or one of his preachers, I hope mostly to find the latter.'

★　★　★

The sorrel was ready for the day, freshly groomed by the kid in the stable, a worn saddle that promised to be gentler on his backside than the new one he had purchased with the horse.

12

Showdown

It was not the best of days for Samuel J. Colston, not a day he was looking forward to. He had been sold out by Washington, no honour among thieves or business men it seemed and through their messenger Billy May, they had made it very clear to him that the play was over and the curtain fallen on the railroad scam. He was on his own and about to lose a great deal of money. The South Texas Railway Company, upon assurances from Sheriff Overmeyer and the county attorney that the troubles around Serenity were under control and now of little consequence, had decided on that route, the cheaper option, and Colfax would be passed by. The result was that the land he and Washington had quietly purchased was pretty nigh on worthless and he would be lucky to recoup ten cents on the dollar, for him a huge personal loss. Washington had sold while the price was still acceptable but they had not informed him of their intentions and he was stuck with it. There was still some small value to the Broken Bow land where the railway needed the right of way, but the new route was mostly over federal territory. The land was probably worth more to him if he stocked it with cattle and kept it as a working ranch. But that was not the whole of it; the county law was asking searching questions as to his involvement in any of the killings and he only had a few answers to those questions. He doubted that anything could be proven against him but it was nevertheless a growing concern and a worry he did not need. He had ended it all, everything except his contact with Aaron Gumm, a contact he had been smart enough to keep at a distance, humouring the assassin with a black spot death code and never actually meeting him face to face, except for the one time when he had first hired the killer. Big problem for him was that he had absolutely no idea as to the whereabouts of the man in order to cut all ties with him.

No, the morning, as bright and warm as the summer sun was, was a dark day both for him and Broken Bow. He set a small wooden table and chair on the veranda and placed a black tin money box, a ledger and the few papers he would need upon it. Just behind him to his left stood the young cowboy Kip Tullet and his older brother Jason and on the other side Howard Smith, each man cradling a sawn-off shotgun close to their bodies. Satisfied with the arrangement, he nodded to the younger man to signal the Chinese cook to hit the cook shack triangle, which would call the gathering of the majority of the ranch hands to the meeting he had informed them would take place that morning. They emerged from the bunkhouse unhurriedly, guessing, he supposed, that the news would not be good. Ten of them in all, including the bruised and still a little bloodied Chet Baker.

Colston cleared his throat and moved to the front of the raised porch. 'Sorry to say, boys, that Broken Bow is cutting back on riders. Kip here, his brother and Howie Smith will be staying on as will the cook and the three Mex hands but as for the rest of you, most were not hired as cowhands but for security, a security no longer needed.' Colston liked the use of the word 'security'; it had a ring of legitimacy about it. 'You can draw your pay here in silver coin and take whatever horse you need, I will give you a bill of sale right here and now to cover that. I would suggest you ride clear of Serenity and maybe head for Colfax or directly for the border. Ride safe and thank you.' He sighed deeply, turned back to the table and sat behind it counting out the money owed, getting each man to sign for the cash and the issued bills of sale for the horses. Some said thank you, a couple shook his hand but most, resigned to a period of unemployment, merely nodded.

Chet Baker was the last man to the table. 'Why them, Mr Colston?' he asked, his voice surly and irritable, indicating the Tullet brothers and the young Smith. 'I was here before them, usually first in last to leave.'

'I know, Chet, and I am sorry but you have too much history here, if the shit hits the fan as is likely, there will be nothing I can do. Best that you be well south of here before Overmeyer shows.'

'This all down to that old lawman Fanning, I suppose?'

'In part but not all, there have been far-away influences afoot here of which you have no knowledge and are not of your concern.' He pushed a small pile of silver coins toward Baker. 'You will see I have given you a small bonus not afforded the other hands because of the injuries you have sustained in my employ. Take it and ride hard and fast,

Chet, and good luck to you.' He pushed the chair back and climbed wearily to his feet, collected the ledger and the tin money box, nodded to Kip Tullet and went inside to the cool darkness, a whiskey bottle and an uncertain future.

Baker watched him go, gave Kip Tullet a dark look and stomped off in the direction of the bunkhouse passing a couple of riders already on their way south and as far from Broken Bow as they could ride on that day. They nodded but he ignored them. He had a plan of his own, no border for him — at least not until he had settled his score with Jack Fanning; it might take a few days but it would come. He packed his warbag and picked up a few supplies from the cookhouse, chose the best horse he could from the remuda and headed toward the trail from Serenity turning off by a rocky gulley, taking high ground and settling himself in a position he had scouted whilst recovering from his still very apparent injuries. The nose was less swollen but still gave him a lot of pain and the ear bled almost every time he slapped his hat on his head without thinking.

It was a good spot, mostly sheltered from the hot afternoon sun, offering even more shelter under a large rocky overhang should it rain and beneath which a small spring bubbled up through the shale. Best of all, it overlooked the easiest of the several trails leading to Broken Bow from Serenity, along which he was pretty certain that one day very soon a certain lawman would be headed. He settled himself on a flat rock, set his Henry rifle on the ground in front of him, rolled a quirly from a full cotton sack of Bull Durham and wondered how to spend the fifty or so dollars Colston had given him when he eventually rode clear of Belstone County for the Mexican side of the Rio Bravo.

And that was what he was still thinking on when he heard the faint rustle of falling shale somewhere behind him. He had the trail to his roost pretty well covered so he was guessing it was a critter, a coyote maybe or even a bird scrabbling for water. He turned slowly and was startled to see standing there, his back to the setting sun and silhouetted by its red glow, a tall, elderly man dressed in black, a preacher in a long, tattered frock coat and flat brimmed hat. 'Where the hell did you spring from, preacher?'

'Wrong place, wrong question.' The man had a deep and sonorous voice, the words pressed out around yellow teeth.

'Best you beat it then, old man, I don't have time for your Bible thumping this day.'

'You do not have any time left at all, Mr Baker.' The man took a step closer and settled his footing on solid rock.

'Excuse me?'

'I believe you heard me perfectly clearly.'

'How the hell do you know my name? We met before?'

'I don't think so, have we?'

'You are damned right we have not, now get your raggedy ass gone.'

'Another day, another time that would have been the right answer and I would have walked away. Any other day that is, but not today.'

'You stink awful bad, best you leave before I lose my temper.' Baker set himself to draw, he was not a fast gun but he reckoned he could take an unarmed man of the cloth or at least scare the old man into leaving.

'I am sorry that you are in the wrong place at the wrong time as you are worth absolutely nothing to me.' As he spoke the frock coat swung open and the man in black raised a sawed-off shotgun he had been holding beneath its skirt, lifting the gun with one hand and pulling both triggers as the stubby twin barrels levelled themselves on Baker's chest. The impact knocked the big man off his feet, blowing him backwards and down into the gully.

Aaron Gumm walked to the edge of

the incline and stared down at the fallen Baker. Flecks of blood rapidly growing in volume stained his lips as he tried to form a word. Gumm knelt down, listening.

'Why?'

'Because Jack Fanning is mine and mine alone and you can have no part of him but, if it helps, you can be assured I will put him down very soon, perhaps even tomorrow.'

If Chet Baker heard or understood that answer, that realisation died with him there in the gully, his big hands clutched against his chest in some last feeble effort to stem the flow of blood brought forth by the heavy charge of double-ought buckshot.

Gumm extracted the spent cartridges and tossed them down on top of the dead man. One orange hull stuck to the blood, the other rolled away and with a hollow sound, clattered across the shale and deep into the dry wash.

★   ★   ★

While Baker lay breathing his last there on the rocky hillside, Jack Fanning was three miles away, riding a small game trail that showed the sign of a heavier footfall than that of a coyote or deer.

Fanning had watched the old line shack from afar, using good cover to hide any movement and using his US Army-issue field glasses he watched for any sign of the old man. Towards dusk he gave up; if Gumm was coming that evening then it would be after dark and his knowledge of the terrain would put him at a distinct advantage over the lawman. He withdrew deep into the woods, had a cold supper washed down with warm spring water from his canteen and settled himself into his blanket, not even venturing to roll a cigarette in case the smoke should alert his quarry.

The next morning, feeling certain he was alone and after an hour or so observing the shack, Fanning broke cover and walked the sorrel around to the rear of the property looking for any sign to indicate the direction the occupier might have come or gone. Towards midday he found it; a game trail, perhaps a coyote or deer or something larger. The trail appeared to be more than that used by an animal. Here and there a heavier foot had trodden the grass, not a horse but a man walking, perhaps. It was all that Fanning had so he went with it, following slowly, leading his horse and at times leaving the trail, circling to pick it up again a couple of hundred or so yards from where he had left it. This was merely a precaution in case he was the quarry and not the hunter. He was wondering if it were a wild goose chase or not and thinking perhaps he would be better off watching the line shack when the sorrel snorted, shook its head and stopped dead in its tracks. Fanning sensed it as well, a pungent smell, the familiar stink recalled from way back and more recently in the shack itself. The stink of Aaron Gumm. Fanning hobbled the sorrel in the long grass, showing greener now as they approached the damp upper reaches of the Serenity River itself.

After fifteen minutes or so, the trail opened up on a narrow grass-covered clearing and to the entrance, almost hidden by bracken, of a lichen-covered cave. Fanning settled himself to wait, then when there was no apparent movement, he ventured upward and into the shadowy darkness of the cave. There was the stink again, stronger than ever. The only furniture a rough wooden table upon which lay a soiled copy of the *Serenity Sentinel*, the issue in which Louise had mapped out his career for the Serenity townsfolk, a Bible, some empty cans and beneath it a bedroll he had no wish to examine. In the furthest and darkest corner of the cave he found a leather gun case and the Sharps rifle together with a reloading press and empty brass, .50 calibre shells waiting for powder and priming caps. The find unnerved him a little as in all probability it meant

Gumm would not leave his weapon of choice for too long. Fanning returned to the entrance and studied the landscape before slipping out of the dank, cold cave and into the warm sunlight. There was no sign of movement and even the crows, inhabitants of such a wilderness, were quiet, their cawing stilled. Convinced he was alone, he moved to the edge of the clearing, turning back toward the cave trying to figure out the best place from which to observe the entrance but where he would not be observed by anyone approaching the cave from the same direction he had. He caught the stink of the man before the rasping voice filtered into his roaring brain, stupid, careless beyond belief.

'You were very careless, Jack Fanning, I expected more of you. Turn around now, very carefully, your hands far away from your weapon.' The old man stood there, a cocked Colt in his hand pointed directly at Fanning's chest. 'I knew it was you, Jack, soon as I saw those scars on your back when you were skinny dipping with your whore. I could have killed you then or many times since then from ambush. No good, sir, I wanted to . . . needed to, watch you die. I wanted so much for you to know it was me.'

Behind the man was a patch of disturbed soil, the grass and leaves removed from its wood covering as it slid from the board that had hidden the spider hole. An Apache trick; bury yourself until the troopers rode past then attack them from behind at the very same moment the Apache they were tracking turned to fight, meaning the surprised soldiers came under fire from both the front and the rear. He had seen the results of such an ambush and in fact had lead the burial party sent to retrieve the American dead.

The front of the old man's trousers were stained and wet with urine. Fanning guessed he had been enclosed in his hideaway for some time, not venturing out until he was certain his victim was under his gun.

'You still stink, old man, or do you prefer to be The Deacon on some mission from a God who would disown you in a heartbeat?' Fanning pitched his voice to match that of Gumm.

'I admire your bravado, Jack.' The yellow teeth bared. 'I would have expected no less of you. I work His ministry, I serve Him, I kill the killers and the worthless trash who pay me to kill are only paying me to do that for which I was chosen.'

'Chosen? You were chosen?'

'That morning you came to see me, ask help of my ministry, a red-eyed and lost youth, that was my beginning, that you so easily took the lives of two worthless people and suffered no loss yourself was my revelation, I realised how easy it would be to rid the world of people of little consequence and be paid for it — both here and later in Paradise itself.' The pistol in the dark man's white hand did not waver but held firm, its muzzle never wavering

240

from Fanning's chest. 'I never expected to see you again, I hope you have had a good life.'

'Did you enjoy the dog, did he hunt well for you?' Fanning was stalling, playing for time; time to do what he did not know. The man could have as easily killed him as talk to him, so he guessed it was some need in Gumm for recognition. An appreciation, a validation of his skill and cunning and a knowledge of his so-called mission for God.

The two men stood there in the shadow of the clouded sky, each with his own thoughts. Aaron Gumm wanting to kill but holding back, savouring the moment; Rio Jack Fanning hanging onto life for a few seconds more.

'I ate the damned dog, killed it with a sledge as soon as you were out of sight. Killed it, cooked it and ate it to the bone. Never did say a word over those graves you dug. Did you enjoy the army, Jack? I read in your whore's paper that you fought side by side with the Federals and that snake Grant.'

'Shiloh, Vicksburg right through to Appomattox.'

'Such a waste.'

'You gave up on God?'

'No and he never gave up on me. I learned a new trade, killing — killing for money, big money, killing in His name. You know how easy it is to kill, Jack, you remember your first, don't you?'

Fanning did not reply and let the silence hang there, feeling the blood flow to his right arm, gauging the distance between them.

Gumm broke the silence. 'The young you, back in the hollows, the girl and man you killed, you remember them? Yes, you do, I can see it in your eyes. A long journey but we both end up here, both maybe sent here to enlighten this godforsaken place . . . me in my way, you in yours.'

'That was thirty years ago. You are an old man damned near seventy, I can smell the years on your breath, on your clothes, you have been alone too long, time to rest,' Fanning said, his voice only a little above a whisper.

'For you Jack, yes, but not for me, not for a long while yet, I have contracts to fulfil.'

'Haven't you heard? They have all been cancelled, Colston is busted, probably in jail right now.'

'You, sir, are lying.'

Noting the first merest hint of uncertainty in Gumm's voice, Fanning pulled. It was the fastest draw he had ever made; it had to be, the big man's gun was cocked and pointing, all that was needed was a slight pressure on the trigger but Gumm, needing to speak with him, to preach at him, to remind him of his long gone days, had waited a fraction of a second too long. Fanning went for the heart but Gumm's extended Colt was between them and the bullet glanced off the side of the weapon just as Gumm squeezed the trigger. The firearm's damaged action caused the capped round to explode in the cylinder shattering his big hand to the wrist before, still with some considerable force, travelling on and burying itself deep in the old man's chest. Staring in disbelief at his bloody, shattered hand, Aaron Gumm sank forward and onto his knees, kneeling there as if in prayer before toppling over sideways and rolling onto his back, staring up at the sky beyond Fanning's shoulder, blood seeping through the yellow teeth, giving the man's mouth an unholy colour.

Out of habit, Fanning kicked the ruined Colt clear before kneeling down beside the fallen man. 'You waited too long, Gumm, hubris, you just had to hear yourself, you murdering son of a bitch, you should have stuck to the shadows, bushwhacking from afar, that was your style.'

Gumm tried to form words through the blood and whispered clearly before dying, 'I am but a voice in the wilderness.'

'You sure as hell are now, you piece

of crap.' Fanning stood up, raised the Colt and hitting the hammer with the heel of his hand, fired a single round into Aaron Gumm's forehead, just a little above the bridge of his nose.

Fanning swore under his breath, his hands trembling as they had after the Serenity shoot-out with Chet Baker, rodding out the spent round and reloading before holstering the Colt, watching as the light went out from the dark eyes, the look of surprise settling there for all eternity as Aaron Gumm, late of the hollows of Kentucky and more recently, Belstone County, stared into the black abyss of the big nowhere.

Epilogue

Rio Jack Fanning, sometime lawman and gunfighter, made his way back to the cabin where he suspected Aaron Gumm had killed the settler Stephen Monroe. The long, thin blade of the knife he had found tucked into the back coat collar of the dead madman's frock coat fitted the description of the wound given by Doc Henderson. It was over; a long-ago dead past was buried along with the so-called Deacon in a shallow grave that had been the man's last hiding place and from which he could so easily have bushwhacked Fanning had he not wanted to gloat, a hubris that had cost him his life. He supposed the coyotes or bears would find him eventually and dig him up, eat what they could and leave the rest for the black crows. A fitting end.

He lit a fire in the potbellied stove

and cooked the last of his rations, washed down by a shot of whiskey taken on the front porch with a freshly rolled quirly between his lips; the last one, he promised himself. He would head back for Serenity at first light, marry Louise, maybe stand for election and grow old gracefully. The times they were rapidly changing and the army Colt .45 with its wired back trigger would no longer be the essential tool in the winning of what was left of the South Texas wilderness.

He slept fitfully that night, imagining Stephen Monroe working the land, losing his wife and then his life, walking the yard, his clothes on fire and screaming at the injustices of life. But more than the spirit of the Scot settler walked through Fanning's dreams and, rolled in his blanket on the cabin floor, he fancied he could smell the stink of the old man who thought himself on some ministry of God. The yellow teeth were bared and the black eyes blazing with fire as he snarled at the man who had dared to take his life. Fanning knew he would dream of Aaron Gumm on and off for the rest of his life and somehow he did not mind that fact. It would serve him well as a reminder of the frailty of man and of his belief in the nearness or the meaning of a real or imagined God.

The morning dawned brightly, the merest promise of rain on the gentle breeze drifting down over the high ground to the west of Serenity River and the dead Deacon's cave. He rode the sorrel at a canter most of the way, resting only briefly on the low rise above Serenity, the township below settled peacefully in front of him as was, he hoped, his future there.

Later that evening in the quiet of the house on Saddlebrook Creek Road with its clear spring water chuckling by, he held the woman close, told her of Aaron Gumm and the reason for the long-ago visit to Trencher's Hollow in Kentucky and the killing of the man in the green hills of the upper Serenity River. She

Other titles in the
Linford Western Library:

SILVER GALORE

John Dyson

The mysterious southern belle, Careen Langridge, has come West to escape death threats from fanatical Confederates. Is she still being pursued? Should she marry Captain Robbie Randall? The Mexican Artiside Luna has his own plans ... With gambler and fast-gun Luke Short he murders Randall's men and targets Careen. Can the amiable cowboy Tex Anderson and his pal, Pancho, impose rough justice as with guns blazing they go to Careen's aid?

CARSON'S REVENGE

Jim Wilson

When the Mexican bandit General Rodriguez hangs Carson's grandfather, the youngster vows revenge, and with that aim joins the Texas Rangers. Then as Carson escorts Mexican Henrietta Xavier to her home, Rodriguez kidnaps her. The ranger plucks the heiress from the general's clutches, and the youngsters make a desperate run for the border and safety. Will Carson's strength and courage be enough to save them as he tries to get the better of the brutal general and his bandits?

listened intently and asked him quietly if all of the violence and the killing had really been worth the building of a railroad.

Rio Jack Fanning thought about that for a long moment before replying then saying simply, 'It was what it was, Louise.'

Some call her Red Kenyon the Red Canyon hellcat — and the young woman with an unmanageable tangle of red hair has proved herself the equal of most men on more than one occasion. But Red is only beginning to realize her mistake in trying to go after the stolen heifers alone. Far from any possibility of rescue, Leif Mortenson leers at the disarmed and helpless nemesis who has twice thwarted him. As panic and despair wash over her, Red knows she has the toughest fight of her life ahead . . .

SALOON

Owen G. Irons

Diane Kingsley, part-owner of the Cock's Crow Saloon, has made one too many enemies, and finally they've seen to it that she was thrown aboard a westbound train and sent out alone into the desert. Well . . . not quite alone, for, when she arrives, she finds that she has been riding with Walt Cassidy, who has also been run out of Sand Hill, for shooting the man who killed his horse. Walt is desperate — and intrigued by Diane's plan to build a saloon in an empty land . . .

GUNS OF SANTA CARMELITA

Hugh Martin

When former deputy town marshal Frank Calland helps out another saddle-tramp whom he finds stranded without food or water in the Arizona desert, he ends up being pursued by an angry posse — but this is only the beginning of his problems. He finds himself donning the lawman's star once more, this time as deputy to Marshal Bill Riggs, who seems to be hiding a dark secret from his past. Calland is thrown into the deep end, and must take responsibility when a band of ruthless outlaws arrives, blood-thirsty for revenge . . .

DEATH CAME CALLING

Adam Smith

Sheriff Ray Cairney is sure something untoward is going on in Bristow, and that Curtis Waring, bank manager and town council leader, is behind it. The arrival of two gunslingers and the subsequent turn of events convince Cairney his hunch was right — but how to prove it? Those involved are rich and powerful, and he is just one man. That, however, won't stop him. The murder of an entire family gives Cairney the evidence he will need to bring justice to Bristow — but it will be a long, hard journey.

FEAR VALLEY

Alex Frew

When a gang of criminals commits an atrocious robbery in the bank of Harrisville, bounty hunter Jubal Thorne is quick on their trail. The murder of innocent bystanders during the robbery makes Thorne, known as Blaze, determined that the criminals will pay with their lives. The maverick leader of the group, Shannon, gives the rest of his men the slip, escaping to Fear Valley at the very end of the desert frontier. The valley is ruled by Valquez, a despot, and soon Blaze the hunter finds himself becoming the prey . . .

TWO GUNS WEST

Neil Hunter

When Bodie and Brand arrive in San Francisco, searching for a kidnapped young woman, the city by the bay doesn't exactly welcome them with open arms. But danger has never stopped these two before — not even when it comes in the form of a deadly Chinese Tong determined to extend its opium empire as far as the east coast. With the help of Captain Richard Hunt, a British agent from Jamaica, all they have to do is bring the Tong — and its murderous criminal contact Milo Traeger — down . . .